An Incorrect Solution

Book 5 in **The Math Kids** *Series*

The Math Kids series
Have you read them all?

An Incorrect Solution

Book 5 in **The Math Kids** Series

by

David Cole

COMMON DEER PRESS

Published by Common Deer Press Incorporated

Published in 2021 by Common Deer Press
1745 Rockland Avenue
Victoria, British Columbia
V8S 1W6

This book is a work of fiction. Names, characters, places and
incidents are either the product of the author's imagination or
are used fictitiously.

Library of Congress-in-Publication Data
Cole, David. – First edition
The Math Kids: An Incorrect Solution / David Cole
ISBN: 978-1-988761-60-2 (print)
ISBN: 978-1-988761-61-9 (e-book)

Cover Image: © Shannon O'Toole
Book Design: David Moratto
Printed in Canada

www.CommonDeerPress.com

*To Stephanie, Jordan, and Justin—The world is,
and will be, better because you are a part of it.*

Chapter 1

Low, dark clouds spit angry drops of rain onto the pavement, where they splattered into growing puddles of muddy water. Justin Grant kept his head down and plodded on toward school, trying to keep up with the much longer stride of Jordan Waters, his best friend since kindergarten.

Truth be told, neither was in much of a hurry to get to McNair Elementary. That was unusual, because both were good students and normally loved school, especially since they had formed the Math Kids club with Stephanie Lewis. The three had solved the mystery of the neighborhood burglars together, but the club had become complete when they'd added Catherine Duchesne. With their new club member, they had solved the mystery of a bank robbery and found a fortune in gold that had helped the town recover from financial hardship. They had also come in second in the district math competition.

But that was all in fourth grade. Now they were

moving to fifth grade and things were changing—and not for the better.

For one thing, Catherine and Stephanie were going to be in a different classroom. The girls were going to be in Mrs. Wilson's class while the boys were going to be in Mr. Miller's. His nickname was "Miller the Killer" because he was so hard on kids. Some of the kids thought their fourth-grade teacher, Mrs. Gouche, had been tough too—they had called her Mrs. Grouch when she was mad—but the word was that Mr. Miller was much, much worse.

But that wasn't what was bothering Jordan about their new teacher. It was math. Mr. Miller hated math. He had the only classroom in the entire school who didn't have a math team in the school-wide competition. Mr. Miller loved English and social studies but made it clear that math was his least favorite subject. Jordan did great in math, but he struggled with English. He hated reading, mixed up letters when he tried to spell, and couldn't stand writing papers. Mr. Miller was going to be his worst nightmare.

"This is going to be a lousy year, isn't it?" Jordan said as he used his long legs to step over a puddle in a low spot in the sidewalk.

"Yeah," replied Justin glumly. He didn't even bother to try to step over the puddle. He was one of the shortest kids in his grade and he knew his short legs weren't going to reach from one side to the other. He just plowed through the puddle, splashing water everywhere. He was glad he had worn an old pair of tennis shoes and not the new ones his mom had bought him.

"It's going to stink not having Stephanie and Catherine in the same class," Justin said as he shook water from one leg.

"Wouldn't really matter, since Mr. Miller hates

math anyway," Jordan said. "I heard he doesn't even have math groups."

Justin didn't reply, just trudged through the rain in his soaked sneakers. The first day of fifth grade was already miserable and they hadn't even reached the school.

***

Four blocks away, Stephanie ducked her head and raced down the sidewalk and into the waiting dryness of Catherine's dad's car.

"Thanks so much for driving us to school, Mr. Duchesne," Stephanie said politely, shaking a few drops of water out of her ponytail onto the floor in the back seat.

"Happy to do it," Mr. Duchesne answered. "It's right on my way to the college anyway, so it's really no trouble. Besides, I still owe you one, don't I?"

Stephanie smiled as she remembered meeting Catherine and working with the other Math Kids to solve the cryptic message Mr. Duchesne had left after he had been kidnapped. Teamwork and their math skills had helped them rescue their new friend's father.

"Hey, check this out!" Catherine exclaimed. "My dad has a new book!" Catherine was positively beaming as she held it up for Stephanie to see.

Mr. Duchesne taught math at the college and had a whole library of math books, many of which he had written himself. Stephanie thumbed through the book, not understanding any of the equations but envious that Catherine's dad was so into math. *She is so lucky*, Stephanie thought to herself.

"Congratulations!" she said. "I think it'll be a while before anything in the book makes any sense to me, but I can't wait to read it when it does."

Mr. Duchesne chuckled from the front seat.

Stephanie placed her gym bag on the seat next to her. If the rain stopped in time, maybe her soccer team would still be able to practice after school. Soccer was one of the few things in the world that Stephanie liked as much as math—well, almost as much. Catherine looked longingly at the bag containing Stephanie's soccer shorts, T-shirt, and sneakers. *I wish I could play soccer like Stephanie*, she thought.

"I can't believe they split us up into two different classrooms," Stephanie said.

"Yeah, it really stinks. Does that mean we'll have to be on a different math team for the district competition?"

"Worse. It means we'll actually have to compete against each other in the school contest," Stephanie said gloomily.

"We'll beat them, of course, but it won't be nearly as much fun," Catherine said.

Catherine smiled to show she was only joking, but Stephanie was worried. Would this be the end of the Math Kids?

Chapter 2

"Hang up your backpacks and quickly find your seats," Mr. Miller said. Having to sit in assigned seats was a change Justin didn't like. He'd been in the same class as Jordan for five years and they'd always been able to sit next to each other. Now they were seated in alphabetical order, with Justin in the front row and Jordan stuck in the back corner. Justin got situated at his desk and looked around the room. He didn't see Susie McDonald, so that was at least a plus. Susie was a drama queen and was always crying about something.

There was a scuffle at the doorway and Justin's heart sank as he watched Robbie Colson push aside a smaller fifth grader and stomp into the room. Justin hadn't seen Robbie since the end of school, and it looked like he had grown another two or three inches since. Justin sighed. He hadn't grown a bit over the summer. Robbie tossed his backpack onto a hook from four feet away, earning him a high five from Hakim Omani and a look of disapproval from Mr. Miller.

"Find your desk, Robbie," he said. Robbie gave an innocent grin and slid into his seat. Justin looked up at Mr. Miller. He was tall and thin and very pale. He was wearing a dark suit and if he didn't move, he could easily be mistaken for someone lying in a coffin. He had thinning black hair and a brown mole under one eye. He was rubbing his hands together and one side of his mouth curled into a half smile. It looked like he was plotting something evil in his mind.

Mr. Miller looked over the classroom, taking a long time to look at each student in turn, all without saying a word. It was kind of creepy, and Jordan's premonition about this being a lousy year was starting to look pretty accurate.

"Okay, let's settle down. I'm Mr. Miller. Your older brothers and sisters may have called me Miller the Killer." There was a smattering of laughter. "If I hear that from anyone in this classroom, it will cost you a week of recess." The laughter was quickly stifled.

"I don't tolerate nonsense in my classroom. This is fifth grade, and it is time for you to begin using proper decorum." Justin let out a groan. Mr. Miller stopped talking and stared at him, his mouth a thin line. Justin looked down at the notebook on top of his desk until Mr. Miller continued. "This year we will write. We will write a lot."

Justin ventured a quick glance back at Jordan, whose face said it all. Jordan hated writing.

"Our focus will be on history, English, and reading," Mr. Miller continued.

Jordan raised his hand hesitantly.

"Yes, Jordan?"

"What about math?"

"We'll do math, as well. Our focus there will be on the basics, multiplication, division, and fractions."

"But Mrs. Gouche—"

"Mrs. Gouche is no longer your teacher. Our focus this year will be on history, English, and reading. For math, we will do exactly what is outlined in the curriculum." He paused to look directly at Jordan. "And nothing more."

Jordan lowered his hand, his face glum. Everything his sister had told him was true. Mr. Miller hated math. It was going to be a long year.

***

Things weren't starting off very well in Mrs. Wilson's fifth grade class either. The morning had been fine but midway through the afternoon the classroom turned into a scene of chaos. It started, unsurprisingly, with the bullies. Even though Robbie, the leader of the group, was in Mr. Miller's room, Mrs. Wilson had gotten the rest of Robbie's crew. The bullies loved to pick on anyone smaller than them, which meant almost everyone. This time, though, the bullies had turned their aggression toward each other.

It all started with Dylan Carmen, a new kid in school who had already shown he was going to fit in well with the bullies. He was a big guy, not quite as big as Robbie but he had a wiry toughness to him. Dylan tripped Bryce Bookerman as he walked in front of his desk. Bryce fell headlong into Brian Brown, knocking his water bottle over and spilling water all over the comic book he was reading behind his social studies book. Brian jumped to his feet with a roar. He took a wild swing at Bryce but hit Dylan instead. Dylan went down hard, knocking over Brian's desk. Now everyone in the classroom was up and out of their seats, some to get out of the bullies' way and others to get closer to see the action.

"That's enough!" shouted Mrs. Wilson to no effect. The class was still in an uproar. Two desks had been knocked over and the bullies were now in a heap of writhing arms and legs as they wrestled each other. Mrs. Wilson waded into the pile, grabbing Bryce by one arm and dragging him to the side.

"Don't move!" she said to him, pointing a finger just inches from his face. Next, she grabbed Brian, pulling him from beneath Dylan's leg and depositing him next to Bryce.

"Sit!" she said firmly, as if Brian were a misbehaving dog. This caused Bryce to let out a laugh, which drew a stern look from the teacher.

"I said that's enough!" she shouted once more, and the class finally went silent. Dylan and Bill froze in place, their arms and legs still entangled.

Mrs. Wilson's face was a bright red and she was struggling to maintain her control as she looked down at the bullies.

"You four, follow me!" she commanded, then she turned and without looking back led them out of the classroom. The bullies followed, but not before Dylan gave Brian one more shove, threatening to start the whole fight over again. Brian managed to restrain himself and followed the others out into the hallway, muttering under his breath.

It was twenty long minutes before Mrs. Wilson returned to the classroom. She seemed very calm and even gave the class a smile when she walked in.

"Well, I think that was quite enough excitement for one day, don't you think?" she asked. "We only have forty minutes left until the bell rings, so please pick a book and we'll have silent reading for the rest of the day."

The remaining time passed in silence. Stephanie read a few chapters in a new book her mom had bought her. It was called *Girls Think of EVERYTHING*. It was full of stories about inventions created by women. Stephanie had one story she was going to show to Justin at lunch. She knew he would appreciate it because it was about Ruth Wakefield's invention of the chocolate chip cookie. Catherine looked through a book of math puzzles, scribbling numbers and equations on a sheet of scratch paper as she worked. The bullies didn't come back to the classroom.

When school ended, Catherine and Stephanie ran to catch up with Justin and Jordan.

"Hey, wait up!" Catherine called.

Jordan turned, and the girls could tell the day had not gone well.

"That bad, huh?" Stephanie asked.

"Worse," Jordan said glumly.

"He's thinking about asking his parents if he can homeschool this year," Justin said.

"At least I could do some math at home."

"How's Mrs. Wilson?" Justin asked.

"Too soon to tell, but okay so far, I guess," Stephanie responded.

Catherine went on to explain about the afternoon fight in the class. "It was total chaos," she said. "There were desks flying everywhere."

"Wow, and that was without Robbie," Justin said.

"No Robbie, but we've got the whole rest of the gang," Catherine said. "At least you only have to deal with one of them."

"Yeah, but Robbie is a handful all by himself," Justin said.

"Why do you think he acts like that?" asked Stephanie.

"I think he got dropped on his head a few too many times as a baby," Justin quipped.

Everyone but Jordan laughed. He was lost in his thoughts of the miserable new school year.

Chapter 3

The next morning, the bullies were back in Mrs. Wilson's class, but they seemed quieter than usual. Brian's eye was bruised, and Bryce had several bandages on his arm where he had scraped it against a desk during the near riot in the classroom the previous day. Catherine wondered what kind of punishment they had received. They were used to being in detention, but she had a feeling this time they were going to get something worse.

"Normally, we would break into our reading groups at this time," started Mrs. Wilson, "but since we got some extra reading time yesterday afternoon, we're going to try something different this morning."

She had the class divide into groups of four. That would have been a no brainer for Stephanie and Catherine the previous year. The Math Kids had stuck together through thick and thin. This year, though, they had to look around the room for two more people.

"Looking for someone to join your group?" Ally Brooks asked in her squeaky voice. Her twin sister, Vivie, was right next to her. Though the girls were identical in looks, they could not have been any more different in personality. Ally was outgoing and loud while her sister was quiet and shy. One day they were best of friends and the next they were bitter opponents. Today they seemed to like each other, with Ally resting her hand lightly on Vivie's shoulder.

Catherine looked at Stephanie.

Stephanie shrugged. The four girls pushed desks together in the front corner of the room. Surprisingly, the bullies formed their own group even though they had been throwing punches at each other only yesterday. Susie McDonald and her friends formed a group and were soon arguing over who should be the leader of the group.

If history is any indication, Susie will win that battle, Catherine thought.

When all the groups had been formed, Mrs. Wilson gave each person two poker chips, one white and one black. "Okay, everyone," she said, "we're going to play a cooperation game. We will play three rounds. The winner will be the team who accumulates the most points. In each round, every person will decide whether to hide a white chip or a black chip under their hand.

Here are the rules on how many points you will earn in each round."

She wrote the rules on the board.

1) *If everyone on the team selects a white chip, everyone on the team wins 10 points*
2) *If only one person shows a black chip, that person wins 30 points and everyone else on the team wins nothing*
3) *If two people choose black chips, they each win 15 points and everyone else wins nothing*
4) *If three people choose black chips, they each win 10 points and the remaining person wins nothing*
5) *If everyone on the team chooses a black chip, everyone gets zero points*

The winner will be the team with the most total points at the end of 0 rounds.

She gave the class a minute to review the rules, and then asked if there were any questions. When no one raised their hand she said, "Okay, then, you'll have two minutes to discuss which chips you'll each be selecting."

Almost immediately, the arguments began.

"We should all put in white chips," Susie argued.

"But what if you say you're going to and then put in a black instead?" asked Mindy Klinger.

"I told you I was putting in a white one!" Susie said, her voice rising.

The group of bullies was having their own loud discussion. Dylan was half out of his seat, pointing a finger at Bill. "Yeah, well you better put in a white chip," he said threateningly.

"What, so you can hold out on us and get thirty?" Brian asked.

"No, we're all going to put in white chips," Dylan growled.

While the other teams huddled, Stephanie whispered a few words to their team. Ally and Vivie looked confused. Ally started to speak up, but kept her mouth shut when she saw Catherine nod confidently. She and Stephanie had already calculated the best strategy without having to say a word.

"Okay, times up! It's time to decide which chip you're going to choose," Mrs. Wilson said.

Mrs. Wilson watched as Catherine's team revealed their choices. Four white chips. Mrs. Wilson gave ten points to everyone on the team.

Susie's group uncovered two black chips and two white chips. Madison and Lashonna high-fived as they each collected fifteen points. The others frowned when they received nothing.

A loud roar came up from the bullies' group. Dylan had talked everyone into putting in white chips, but he had put in a black one.

"Suckers!" he yelled in triumph as he collected his thirty points.

"I told you that's what he was going to do," complained Brian. He and the other bullies glared angrily at Dylan.

"Cheater!" Bryce and Bill said together.

"That ends the first round," said Mrs. Wilson. "You have two minutes to discuss."

We heard Dylan trying to convince his teammates that this time he really was going to put in a white chip. Based on the conversation, no one on his team appeared to trust him.

There didn't seem to be much trust on Susie's team either. She was upset that two people on her team had defected and was threatening to tell her mom. Susie's mom was the president of the Parent Teacher Organization and liked to throw her weight around with teachers, the principal, other parents, and even students. Madison looked terrified, and Stephanie was certain she was going to put in a white chip this time. She wasn't so sure about Susie though.

"Okay, it's time to make your decision," Mrs. Wilson said loudly.

Once again, with no discussion whatsoever,

Stephanie and Catherine's team hid white chips under their hands. Mrs. Wilson smiled as the team revealed their chips. She gave each person ten points.

As Stephanie suspected, Susie's teammates all put in white chips, while Susie defected and put in a black. She gleefully took her thirty points while the rest of her team got nothing. Dylan and Brian each put in a black and got fifteen points. The rest of the team got nothing, but it was Dylan who was furious.

"You said you were putting in a white, Brian!" he shouted.

"So did you, Dylan," Brian countered.

Bryce and Bill remained silent, but it was obvious they weren't happy with the way things were going.

"Okay, you have two minutes to decide how you want to play in the final round," said Mrs. Wilson.

Once again, Catherine and Stephanie remained silent, watching in amusement as the kids in other teams bickered and tried to convince everyone to put in white chips, knowing all the while that they themselves planned to defect and put in a black so they could earn more points. After two minutes, Mrs. Wilson said it was time to play. Catherine and Stephanie's team once again showed all white chips, and everyone received ten points. The other teams all put in black chips and received nothing.

"Okay, that's the end of the last round, so it's time to count your winnings," Mrs. Wilson announced.

"I got forty-five!" Dylan yelled out, drawing angry looks from the rest of his team. "Does anyone have more than that?"

Mrs. Wilson looked around the classroom. Sure enough, Dylan had acquired more points than anyone.

"Hah!" he said triumphantly. "What do I win, Mrs. Wilson?"

"It's a cooperation game," she reminded the class, "so I need you to count up all of your team's winnings."

Dylan looked confused. "But I got more than everyone," he said. "That means I won, right?"

"You may have more than anyone else, but I'm interested in how many points your team has," the teacher patiently explained.

Dylan's team counted their points. "We got sixty," Dylan announced.

Susie announced that they, too, had collected sixty points as a team.

Mrs. Wilson looked over at Stephanie and Catherine expectantly.

"One hundred and twenty," Stephanie announced.

"What?" Dylan shouted. "That's impossible. They cheated, Mrs. Wilson! I got the most points, so I won."

"Can you explain why you won, Stephanie?" Mrs. Wilson asked.

"It was easy, actually," she replied. "We just calculated the best team winnings for each combination of chips and chose that strategy for each round."

"Wait, you didn't say this was a math problem," Bill complained. "It's not fair to have a bunch of nerds on the same team."

"We don't call each other names, Bill," the teacher scolded, "and it's not really a math problem. The goal of the game was to cooperate, to do what was best for the team, not for yourself. By doing so, these four have each earned ten bonus points on their next test."

The bullies were furious, and Stephanie had a feeling there would be payback for that later, but for the moment the win felt great. Mrs. Wilson might not have thought of the game as math, but Stephanie and Catherine certainly did. They had quickly worked out all the possible combinations, and it was clear how their team should play.

If everyone put in a white chip, the team won forty points. If there was one black chip, the team only won thirty. Two black chips also resulted in winning thirty points for the team, as did putting in three. The worst case was everyone putting in a black chip, in which case the team won nothing.

	Chip color / winnings				
Player 1	○ 10	○ 0	○ 0	○ 0	● 0
Player 2	○ 10	○ 0	○ 0	● 10	● 0
Player 3	○ 10	○ 0	● 15	● 10	● 0
Player 4	○ 10	● 30	● 15	● 10	● 0
Team	40	30	30	30	0

That made the decision simple. The best team strategy was for everyone to put in a white chip every time. Each person would not win as much, but the team won the most each round.

Catherine and Stephanie were still talking about the game, and the bonus test points, as they walked to lunch. They saw Jordan and Justin sitting at a table against the far wall of the cafeteria and joined them.

"Mrs. Wilson is growing on me," Stephanie said as she examined her lunch box. She smiled as she opened a plastic container. "Gulab jamun!"

"A glob of jam?" Jordan asked.

"Gulab jamun," Stephanie laughed. "It's a dessert. My grandma makes them whenever she comes to visit. You'd love 'em. They're sweet dumplings—like an Indian doughnut, only better!"

"Speaking of dessert..." Justin said.

Stephanie smiled as she watched Justin start to eat his cookies, his sandwich untouched.

"You never know how much time we have to live," he explained, "so you might as well eat your dessert first."

"Words to live by," Catherine said as she reached for one of the dumplings.

"Why's Mrs. Wilson growing on you?" Justin asked.

Stephanie explained the cooperation game and how they had figured out the best way to play.

"That would never happen in Mr. Miller's class," Jordan complained. "If it has something to do with math, it's off the table."

"I don't think she intended it as a math exercise," Catherine said.

"So why do you think Mrs. Wilson had us play that game?" Stephanie asked. She suspected that Mrs. Wilson hadn't done it without a reason.

"My dad told me about a game like that called the prisoner's dilemma," Catherine said. "It's about making decisions that help you personally instead of working as a team."

"We should talk about that at our next meeting," Jordan said, his mood instantly brightened by the prospect of doing math. "Does Saturday morning still work for everyone?"

"I might not be able to come," Justin said. "I need to get started on my history paper."

Jordan frowned. Just the thought of writing a paper was bad enough, but when it interfered with the Math Kids, it was even worse.

"What history paper?" Stephanie asked.

"We've got to write a paper on a historical event that happened between 1500 and 1700," Justin said.

"Yeah, and then we have to read it in front of the whole class," Jordan added. "I hate history. I hate writing papers. I hate standing in front of the class. I hate this whole stupid assignment."

"Wow, tell us how you really feel," Catherine teased. Jordan gave her a look, but Catherine smiled to let him know she was just joking.

Stephanie twisted her ponytail, thinking. "Wait a minute," she said. "Maybe it's not as bad as you think."

Justin looked up from his carrot sticks. Jordan quit chewing his cookie, a bit of a chocolate chip hanging from his lower lip. He looked hopeful.

"Can it be *any* historical event?" Stephanie asked.

"That's what Mr. Miller said."

"Well, you know, there were a lot of math events that happened in history," she said, lifting one eyebrow. Jordan's face lit up as he figured out where she was going.

"So instead of a history paper, you're saying I should write a math paper," he said thoughtfully.

"It beats history, right?"

Jordan began to smile. "Yeah, writing a math paper isn't nearly as bad," he said.

Chapter 4

Stephanie and Catherine were greeted by Mr. Duchesne as they walked through the door on Saturday morning. He was reading the newspaper and shaking his head.

"Where's the other half of the Math Kids?"

"Working on a history assignment," Catherine said.

"History? Who cares about history when you could be doing math?" Mr. Duchesne chuckled.

"They said Mr. Miller hates math," Stephanie said.

"Meaning he's a guy who doesn't get math." Mr. Duchesne shook his head. "He's part of the reason we see things like this in the paper." He pointed to the weather for the weekend. "What's the high temperature today?"

"Seventy-six," Stephanie answered.

"And what's the low temperature tomorrow?"

"Eighty-one," she answered. Mr. Duchesne paused while she thought about what she had said. "Wait a minute. The low temperature tomorrow can't be more than the high temperature today. That doesn't make sense. Where did those five degrees go?"

"That's exactly right, Stephanie. It doesn't make mathematical sense. But you see stuff like this all the time. Journalists use millions when they meant billions. Advertisers offer sale prices that are worse than the normal price. And no one seems to notice when the percentages on a poll question add up to more than one hundred."

Catherine nodded. "That could be a topic at our next Math Kids meeting. We could bring in newspapers and find examples of incorrect math."

"It won't be hard to find," Mr. Duchesne said. "There is a lot of bad math out there. It reminds me of one of my favorite jokes."

"Uh oh, here it comes, Stephanie," Catherine said. "Dad joke warning."

Mr. Duchesne smiled but continued anyway. "A visitor asks the museum guard how old the dinosaur skeleton is. The guard answers that it is ninety million and six years old. The visitor wanted to know how he could be so precise with his answer. It's easy, said the guard. They told me it was ninety million years old when I started working here, and that was six years ago."

Stephanie and Catherine laughed.

"I don't think Mr. Miller would get that joke," Mr. Duchesne said.

"I feel really sorry for Justin and Jordan," his daughter responded.

"How come so many people don't get math?" Stephanie asked.

Mr. Duchesne thought for a moment before answering. "I think there is one big reason, Stephanie. It takes a while to learn the fundamentals of math before you can do anything interesting with it. You like to play soccer, right?"

"Yes!"

"I'm not good at it myself, but I love to watch it. That's where it's different than math. You can love soccer without being a good player. Even someone just starting out with soccer can kick the ball in the back yard and enjoy themself. But it's not that easy with math. You must learn quite a bit before it gets to be enjoyable. Addition is boring. Subtraction isn't any better. Multiplication is more interesting, but it's still not something people do for fun. It's not until you get to the point where you can solve real problems that people start to love doing math."

Stephanie nodded thoughtfully.

"And if you never get the fundamentals of math, you're never going to get to the point where you love it,"

Mr. Duchesne continued. "It's unfortunate because you and Catherine understand how math can be fun, but so many other kids don't ever get there."

"That is sad. They don't know what they're missing," Stephanie said. "I can't imagine not being able to do math or play soccer." She looked over at Catherine. "Speaking of which, it's time for your soccer lesson."

Catherine blushed. "Are you serious?"

"Yeah, you always ask about soccer. It's about time you learned to play."

A few minutes later, the girls were laughing as they practiced kicking the ball back and forth to each other in the back yard. Mr. Duchesne watched from the back window, laughing as Catherine completely missed the ball and fell onto her back in the grass.

"Maybe she should stick to math," he said to himself.

***

Jordan did research on his history paper for three hours before he even wrote a single word. He searched website after website looking for historical math topics. Unfortunately, every time he stumbled upon an interesting math subject, he got sidetracked from what he was supposed to be doing. When he finally looked up at the clock on his desk, he saw it was midafternoon and he was starving.

When Jordan walked into the kitchen for some lunch his dad was bent over the table working on a new model ship. He loved to build ships from kits. The den was full of them, everything from submarines to sailboats to a gigantic aircraft carrier with a dozen miniature jets on the deck. When he was younger, Jordan had been fascinated with his dad's hobby, but every time he tried to help, he always ended up gluing the plastic pieces to his fingers instead of the ship.

"What are you building now, Dad?"

"This is a model of a Swedish warship called the Vasa," he answered. Jordan watched as his dad carefully added a cannon to the ship, using a tiny line of glue to hold it in place. Jordan shook his head, thinking about how the glue had always come out in a big glob whenever he had tried.

"That's a lot of cannons," Jordan said.

"The Vasa had twin gun decks, which was unusual in the early 1600s."

"I bet no one wanted to mess with that ship," Jordan said admiringly.

"No one ever did, but not because of the cannons."

"Then why?"

"Because the ship sank before it ever made it out of the harbor," his dad answered.

And with that, Jordan had his topic.

Chapter 5

Jordan was nervous as he reread his history paper for what felt like the hundredth time. He thought the topic, the history of nautical math errors, was interesting, but he was worried Mr. Miller would not like it. One by one, Jordan's classmates had read their papers aloud in front of the class. Mr. Miller had scowled and shaken his head at most of the recitations. He had been especially brutal with his comments on Robbie's paper on the Civil War. Jordan agreed that the paper was awful, and Robbie had struggled with some of the words as he read it. And, of course, the Civil War happened in the 1800s, which wasn't even close to the assignment. Still, he felt Mr. Miller had been too hard on Robbie. It wasn't often Jordan felt sorry for the boy who had made his own life miserable on so many occasions, but this was one of those few times.

Now it was almost Jordan's turn to stand up in front of the class and read his paper.

"Jordan?"

"Huh?"

"Are you ready to present?" Mr. Miller asked.

"Um, sure. I mean, I guess so."

"You don't sound very sure about it."

The class laughed, and Jordan felt his face heating with embarrassment.

Jordan stood, knocking his report off his desk to the floor. There was more laughter as he bent to retrieve the papers. He finally got settled in front of the class and looked up and saw Justin. His friend winked and mouthed, "You've got this." Jordan took a deep breath and began to read.

"My report is called 'The History of Nautical Math Errors.'"

"Figures it would be something about math," someone whispered. Jordan thought it might have been Stan Warwick, but he wasn't certain.

"Please continue, Jordan," Mr. Miller said sharply, his squinty eyes scanning the class.

"In 1491, Christopher Columbus made a math error when he calculated the circumference of the Earth. Everyone knew it was about twenty-five thousand miles around the Earth, but Columbus thought it was only fifteen thousand miles. Because of his mistake, he thought he could reach China by sailing west from Spain. Everyone else going to China had to sail around

Africa and it took a really long time. If Columbus could find a shorter route it would be much less expensive to trade with China. He convinced Queen Isabella of Spain his calculations were right, and they paid for his three ships, the *Nina*, the *Pinta*, and the *Santa Maria*. Columbus set off west to find his way to China using his short cut.

"He didn't make it to China, but Columbus did find some islands in the Caribbean. He thought he had made it to India, so he called the people on the islands "Indians." And even though everything Columbus did was mostly wrong it was a great deal for Spain and Europe because his mistake succeeded in opening the Americas to Europe.

"Here's another math mistake that ended up sinking a ship. In 1628, Sweden launched a new warship called the Vasa. It only sailed for twenty minutes before it sank. Thirty people drowned when the ship went down less than a mile from shore.

"It was more than three hundred years before they were able to raise the Vasa. They restored the ship and it is now in its own museum in Stockholm. The ship was studied by lots of people and they finally figured out what went wrong. The ship builders used two different rulers. One ruler used the Swedish foot, which is twelve inches long. The other ruler used the Amsterdam foot, which is eleven inches long.

"The two different measurements caused one side of the ship to be heavier than the other. This made the ship lean to one side and when it was hit by a gust of wind it tipped over. They had the cannon windows open and the ship quickly filled with water and sank.

"These are two examples of why math is really important, even in history."

Jordan snuck a look over at Mr. Miller. He was frowning and shaking his head.

"Jordan, the assignment was to share an event in history that you found interesting. Instead, it sounds like you are trying to give the class a math lesson."

"I think it's interesting, Mr. Miller," Justin spoke up.

"I don't recall asking for your opinion," Mr. Miller responded. "Whether or not you find it interesting doesn't change the fact the assignment was about history, not math."

"There is a lot of math in history," Jordan argued.

"The assignment was also focused on the years 1500 to 1700," Mr. Miller said. "I believe the line says 'in fourteen hundred and ninety-two, Columbus sailed the ocean blue'."

"Yeah, but he made four voyages," Jordan protested. "I guess you could say 'in fifteen hundred and two, Columbus was still on the ocean blue.'"

Justin snickered. Mr. Miller did not. "Thank you, Jordan, that will be enough."

Jordan slumped back to his desk and slid into his chair. Even though he had worked hard on his paper, he knew he wasn't going to get a very good grade. It was only a week into fifth grade, and things were going downhill fast.

Chapter 6

Jordan was right. His grade on his first history paper was not good. Mr. Miller had written a big *D* at the top of the first page. Misspelled words were circled. Punctuation was added. There were notes written in the margins on both sides of every page. All of it in red ink.

"It looked like my paper was bleeding," Jordan complained to Justin as they sat together at lunch. "And the worst was his final comment. He said my idea for the paper was terrible."

"That doesn't seem fair," Justin said. "I mean, he did say we could write about anything in history."

"I know. I guess I should just stay away from any math topics since he hates math so much."

"Speaking of math, this is the second week of school and we haven't even opened our math book," Justin said.

"My sister had Mr. Miller and said it was like that

the whole year. My dad finally complained to the principal."

"Did it help?"

"Not really," Jordan said. "I guess we'll have to learn math on our own this year. Man, I really miss Mrs. Gouche."

The two boys ate their lunch in silence. Jordan didn't even finish the chocolate chip cookies his mom had packed.

"Well, at least Mr. Miller can't ruin recess," Justin said. "You ready?"

"Actually, he can ruin it," Jordan said. "I've got to write each misspelled word from my paper fifty times."

"Are you kidding me?"

"I wish I was. You go on without me. I'll see you back in class."

"Wait, how many words did you misspell?"

"You don't want to know."

Justin watched as his best friend plodded out of the cafeteria with his head down. Justin sat by himself on a swing in the playground, deep in thought, until the bell rang to return to class.

That afternoon, Mr. Miller had the class open their math books for the first time. Justin stole a glance back at Jordan and mouthed "finally" to his friend.

"Okay class, today we're going to review multiplication of two-digit and three-digit numbers,"

Mr. Miller said in his monotone voice. The class groaned. Mr. Miller ignored them and turned his attention to the board. He worked through a few simple examples without even looking back to see if there were any questions. When he finished, he reached for a stack of papers on his desk.

"I've always found the best way to learn math is through repetition," he said.

"Drill and kill, you mean," said someone from the back of the room. Mr. Miller squinted his eyes and scanned the class, looking for the guilty party. Several students squirmed in their seats, but Mr. Miller wasn't able to determine who had said it.

"There are forty practice problems on this worksheet," he said as he walked through the room handing out the sheets of paper. More groans. I'll give you the next hour and a half to work on these. I will be out of the room for a few minutes, but I'll have Mrs. Sheffield from next door checking in on you, so I expect good behavior while I'm gone."

You couldn't hear anything but the sound of pencils scratching on paper for the next twenty minutes as the class worked on the multiplication problems.

"Psst!"

Justin looked up when he heard the sound, like air leaking from a punctured tire. When it wasn't repeated, he put his head back down and resumed his work.

"Psssssst!"

There it was again. This time when Justin looked over, he could see that it was Robbie who had made the sound. The large boy was staring directly at Justin.

"Yeah, Robbie, what do you need?" Justin asked.

"The answers."

"The answers?"

"Yeah, pass your sheet over so I can copy down your answers."

"They're not hard. Why don't you just do the work?" Justin asked. It was a bold question. Robbie didn't like to be talked back to and there was no teacher in the room to help if things got out of hand.

Robbie said something quietly that Justin couldn't quite hear.

"What did you say?" Justin asked. He took a quick look at the door to the hallway to make sure the coast was still clear.

"I don't get it," Robbie answered.

"Get what?"

"Multiplying numbers with more than one number. The times tables were easy. That was just memorizing. But these are confusing. I can't ever seem to get the numbers lined up right."

"I can help you," Jordan said, coming up the aisle from the back of the room. Robbie sneered.

"Seriously, I can help. Let me show you a different way to do it," Jordan said. He went to the whiteboard to explain. Everyone in the class had stopped working now and all eyes were on Jordan.

"This is called the lattice method of multiplication," he explained. "Let's say we want to multiply 58 times 213. You start by drawing a table with the first number you're multiplying on the top and the second on the right."

He drew a two by three table on the whiteboard.

"We put the 58 at the top and the 213 on the right," he continued.

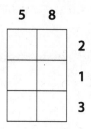

"Now we're just going to do the multiplication of each number. We'll start by splitting each box in the table in two." Jordan drew a diagonal line through each of the boxes.

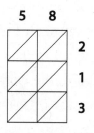

"5 times 2 is 10. We put the 1 in the upper left side of the box and the 0 in the lower right side."

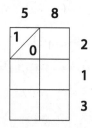

"We do that with each of the boxes. If the answer is less than 10, like 1 times 5, we just put a 0 in the upper left side of the box." Jordan quickly filled in the rest of the boxes.

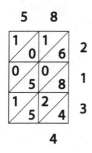

"Easy so far, right?" Jordan asked Robbie.

Robbie nodded. "It's just the times tables. Anyone can do that."

"Now all we have to do is add up the numbers in the diagonals," Jordan said. "We start at the bottom right diagonal. It only has one number, 4, so that one is easy. We put the 4 at the bottom." Jordan demonstrated on the whiteboard.

"Now we add the numbers on the next diagonal," Jordan explained. "5 plus 2 plus 8 is 15. We put the 5 at the bottom and we carry the 1 to the next diagonal." Jordan showed his work on the next diagonal.

"See how I carried the 1?" Jordan pointed out the small number 1 he had placed in the next diagonal. "Then we just keep doing that with each diagonal." He showed the work for the rest of the diagonals.

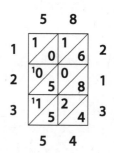

"Now we just read the answer. We start at the top left and just read down and to the right," Jordan said. He pointed at each number as he read the answer. "1, 2, 3, 5, 4, or 12,354."

An excited murmur went through the class. Several students calculated the answer using the more traditional way they had been taught.

"It checks out!" shouted Hakim from the back of the room.

"What checks out?"

The class went deadly silent as all heads pivoted toward the classroom door. Mr. Miller stood there, arms crossed, his pale face tinged with red as he angrily looked at Jordan.

"Um, I was just showing them how to use the lattice method for doing multiplication," Jordan stammered.

"Did I ask you to demonstrate another method?" Mr. Miller asked.

Jordan shook his head, his eyes down.

"Did I ask you to get out of your seat?

Another shake of Jordan's head.

"Then I suggest you return there immediately."

Jordan walked quickly back to his seat.

Mr. Miller looked at the table Jordan had drawn on the whiteboard. He shook his head and emphatically erased it. He turned to face the class.

"I showed you the way to multiply two- and three-digit numbers," he said. "We'll use that method. You'll each be receiving two worksheets to take home. They are due back tomorrow morning." Most of the class looked angrily at Jordan.

"Well, at least I know how to do it now," Robbie said.

Mr. Miller gave Robbie a long look before continuing, "And if you choose to use another method to show your work, I'll mark the answer as incorrect. Now, get out your social studies books and turn to chapter three."

"And Jordan?"

"Yes, sir?"

"Please remain after the class is dismissed for the afternoon."

Chapter 7

"Two weeks of detention?" Justin asked.

"Yeah, my parents are going to kill me," Jordan replied. His head was down, and he looked thoroughly defeated. "And that's before they see the grade I got on my history paper."

"Well, at least they can't kill you twice."

"Yeah, I guess I've got that going for me," Jordan replied. A half smile formed on his face.

They walked in silence, Jordan thinking about the conversation he was going to have with his parents when he got home. Justin had other things on his mind.

"Um, you forget where you live?" Jordan asked.

"Huh?" Justin looked up in surprise. He had been so deep in thought that he had walked right past his own house without glancing up. Jordan had seen this before. He called it Justin's "zone," where his best friend was thinking so hard about something that everything else faded away.

"What are you thinking about, Justin?"

"Nothing, just thinking."

"Really?" Jordan didn't believe his friend, but he also knew he wasn't going to be able to pry anything out of him until Justin was good and ready to tell him. "Well, I guess I'm off to the firing squad."

"The what? Oh, your parents. Yeah, good luck with that," Justin said. He turned back toward his house. "It'll be okay, buddy," he said over his shoulder.

Jordan wasn't so sure. When he got home, his parents weren't there. He was happy to see that, but he knew it was only putting off the inevitable. His older sister, Linda, was sitting on the couch watching music videos on her laptop. She looked up as Jordan entered the living room.

"What's the matter? Somebody beat your high score in *Zombie Attack*?" she asked.

"No, it's worse than that."

"Wow, even worse than getting beat at some stupid video game?"

Jordan reached into his backpack and handed his sister the detention notice from the principal.

"Two weeks? What did you do to deserve that?"

"I taught kids in my class a different way to do multiplication."

She looked at him carefully, trying to figure out if he was kidding. The serious look on his face told her he wasn't. "Why don't you ever listen to anything

I say?" she asked. "I told you Miller the Killer didn't get his nickname by being a nice guy. And I told you he hates math!"

"I know. You were right."

"What? Can you say that again? Is my little brother actually admitting that his sister was right? I have got to write this down in my journal!" She quit teasing when she saw how miserable he looked. "Hey, it'll be fine. Just tell Mom and Dad what happened."

"Tell Mom and Dad what?" Jordan's dad said from the doorway. Neither Jordan nor Linda had heard him come in through the garage.

"It's a long story," Jordan said glumly.

"Sounds like a great dinnertime conversation." The overhead door rumbled from the garage. "I think your mom just got home. How about helping get the table set for dinner?"

Jordan's mom came in through the mudroom carrying a large bag of Chinese food for dinner. It was normally one of Jordan's favorite meals but tonight he just picked at the food on his plate.

"So, what is it you wanted to tell us, Jordan," his dad asked.

"He got two weeks of detention!" Linda blurted out. Her dad gave her a pointed look.

"Jordan, would you like to elaborate on your sister's announcement?"

Jordan took a deep breath and launched into the story, never lifting his eyes from his plate. He didn't get in trouble very often, and he wasn't sure how his parents were going to take this news. He explained about Mr. Miller and how he hated math. He told them about the multiplication worksheet and how he was trying to help his classmates learn a different method for doing the work.

"Isn't it the teacher's job to teach different methods?" his mother asked. Linda snorted, drawing a sharp look from her mom. Linda started to speak but decided it was best to keep quiet. She speared a water chestnut and popped it into her mouth instead.

"I'd be surprised if he even knows another method," Jordan said.

"Two weeks of detention seems like a harsh punishment for trying to help your classmates," Jordan's dad said. "Is there anything you left out?"

Jordan went to the mudroom and opened his backpack. He pulled out his history paper and handed it over without a word. His dad looked at it carefully, reading it from beginning to end without comment. When he had finished, he handed it to Jordan's mom.

"Not a great way to start the new school year," he said. He looked at Jordan with a serious expression on his face.

"I know, but—" Jordan protested. His dad held up a hand to cut him off.

"No buts on this one. I'm willing to cut you some slack on the detention because you had good intentions, but this paper is all on you."

"He hated my subject," Jordan said.

"That may be, but it doesn't explain the spelling and grammar errors, does it?"

Jordan shook his head.

"So, what are you going to do about your situation?" his dad asked.

Jordan scrunched up his face, thinking hard. "There has to be a solution," he said.

"This isn't one of your stupid math puzzles," Linda said.

Jordan glared at his sister, but his expression slowly turned into one of resignation. "Yeah, you're probably right," he said.

"Wait! My brother said I'm right? That's twice in one day!"

Jordan ignored the sarcasm and thought some more. "Still, there has to be some way to fix this."

"Would it help if we set up a meeting with your teacher?" his mother asked.

"No, I've got to figure this one out on my own."

His parents nodded. "Let us know if we can help," his mother said.

"And one other thing," his dad added. "You know there are about a thousand different spell-checking programs out there, don't you?" He gave his son a small smile. "How about using one of them for your next paper?"

Chapter 8

On the way to school the next day, Jordan talked with Justin about his dinnertime conversation.

"I wish it was a math problem," Jordan said. "At least there would be some way to solve it."

"I don't know. Remember Catherine's dad talking about the Millennium Prize problems? Those problems have been unsolved for like forever."

"One of 'em finally got solved, though, didn't it?" Jordan countered.

"Yeah, but Mr. Miller may be an even tougher problem to solve."

"Maybe, but we've got to solve it."

"Do you really think we can get Mr. Miller to like math?" Justin asked.

"I hope so. Otherwise it's going to be an awfully long year."

They turned the corner and started across the playground. They were only fifty yards from the back door of the school when they spotted trouble. Robbie and several of his crew were sitting on top of the monkey bars. It was too late to turn back, so Justin and Jordan adjusted course to steer as far away from the group as they could.

"Going somewhere?" Robbie called out. He hopped down from the bars and quickly closed the distance to Justin and Jordan.

"Just heading to class," Jordan said.

"You know you got me in a lot of trouble with that stunt you pulled yesterday," Robbie said. He stepped in between Jordan and the back door, effectively blocking his way forward.

"I was trying to help."

"Some help. I had to do two multiplication worksheets and ended up with a week of detention."

"What did *you* get detention for? I was the one who was out of my seat."

"Well, according to my detention slip, Mr. Miller doesn't seem to like my attitude," Robbie said.

"We've got something in common, I guess," Jordan said. "He doesn't appreciate my attitude either."

Robbie spoke quietly so his friends couldn't hear him. "Well, for what it's worth, your method for multiplying numbers was pretty cool. Thanks for showing us."

With that, Robbie turned on his heels and walked

into the building, leaving Justin and Jordan to stare after him in shock.

"What was that?" Jordan asked.

"You got me. What do you think got into him?"

"I don't know, but I bet it doesn't last."

"Yeah, you're probably right," Justin agreed.

Mr. Miller was in a lousy mood when Justin and Jordan walked into the classroom.

"You're late!" he snapped.

"But the bell hasn't rung yet," Justin protested. Jordan wisely decided to keep quiet.

"You're supposed to be in your seat ready to learn when the bell rings," Mr. Miller said.

Justin glanced at the clock as he stowed his backpack and walked to his desk. Mr. Miller watched him the entire way. Justin slid into his seat just before the bell rang. "Ready to learn," he said under his breath.

Mr. Miller looked over the class. "Pass your multiplication homework to the front of the row," he said. He watched as Robbie pulled his sheets out of his notebook and passed them forward. When all the homework was at the front, Mr. Miller collected them and placed the papers on his desk.

"This morning we'll be continuing our poetry unit," Mr. Miller said. "I want you to read 'The Road Not Taken' by Robert Frost. Think about what the poet is trying to say in this poem. Pay careful attention to the symbolism and allegory. After you read it, I want you to write a one-page paper discussing the theme of the poem."

Hakim raised his hand. "If we don't like that poem, can we choose a different one?"

"You want a choice?" Mr. Miller asked.

"Yes," Hakim said. Around the classroom, heads nodded in agreement.

"Have you ever heard of a Hobson's choice?" the teacher asked. He looked around but no one had raised their hand. "Thomas Hobson was a stable owner in Cambridge, England, in the seventeenth century. When customers wanted to rent a horse, he gave them the choice of the horse in the stall closest to the door or taking none at all."

"But that means they didn't really have a choice, doesn't it?" Jordan asked.

"That's what a Hobson's choice is: take it or leave it," Mr. Miller smiled.

The class grumbled. In the back of the room, Jordan closed his eyes. He looked like he was in pain. Reading was bad enough, but surely poetry was medieval torture designed by teachers to punish their students.

"Trust me, I'd rather be reading poetry than spending my time recording grades," Mr. Miller said. He opened the laptop on his desk while the class began to read. The frown on his face showed that he meant what he said.

The frown also got Justin thinking.

***

When the final bell rang, Jordan reported to detention. He dropped his backpack on the floor and took a seat. He looked around the room. Robbie was slouched in a chair in the back. He and Dylan Carmen were snickering and passing notes back and forth whenever Coach Baker turned his back. There were two younger kids sitting in the front row, hands folded in front of them as they quietly waited for the hour to pass. Jordan wondered what they had done to earn detention.

With nothing to do to pass the time, he decided he might as well get something accomplished. He pulled his poetry book, a sheet of paper, and a pencil out of his backpack. He read the Robert Frost poem again. Jordan decided it was not as bad as he had imagined it would be. At least it was short.

There was not much plot in "The Road Not Taken," but something in the poem struck a chord with him. The poem seemed to be about a guy trying to choose which road to take through the woods. In the end, the guy chose the "one less traveled" and seemed to think doing so made "all the difference." Jordan thought about that for a while. What was the poet trying to say?

For some reason, Jordan's thoughts went to Mr. Miller. Why did he hate math so much? Of course, Mr. Miller could ask Jordan why he hated to read. That's when it dawned on him. Math to Mr. Miller was like poetry to Jordan. While his teacher knew how to analyze a poem and understood terms like *symbolism* and *allegory*, he didn't know how math could help him in everyday life. Jordan and Mr. Miller had taken different roads through the woods!

Suddenly the poem made sense. It was a challenge to choose your own path. There wasn't a right or wrong road, but whichever one you chose to take, you had to make it your own.

Jordan picked up his pencil and put his thoughts to paper. He was still writing when Coach Baker tapped him on the shoulder. The tip of Jordan's pencil snapped off as he jumped.

"Hey Jordan! It's time to head out, man," Coach Baker said.

Jordan still looked confused.

"Detention is over."

"Oh, right," Jordan said. He was surprised at how fast the hour had flown by. He crammed the paper, pencil, and poetry book into his overstuffed backpack. He left the room with a grin.

The smile faded as he walked out the front door and saw Robbie and his dad. Mr. Colson had pulled his police car into the circle drive in front of the school. Now he was standing toe to toe with Robbie and was waving his arms as he yelled at his son. Even as far away as he was, Jordan could hear every word.

"I told you to be out in front of the school when I got here!" Mr. Colson yelled.

"I got out as soon as I could," Robbie answered.

"I don't have time to wait for you every day just because you can't keep your mouth shut in school. I've got the late shift this week, and I don't need the Lieutenant ripping into me because I'm not there for roll call."

Another wave of Mr. Colson's arms. Jordan noticed that Robbie flinched every time his dad raised a hand.

"It's not my fault, Dad," Robbie said. "Mr. Miller hates me."

"I don't need any lousy excuses, and I don't need you talking back to me," Mr. Colson said. He raised an arm threateningly. Robbie ducked his head and cowered in place. Mr. Colson looked up and saw Jordan. He lowered his arm. "Get in the car," he ordered his son.

They both got in the squad car and Mr. Colson drove off, but not before giving a long look in Jordan's direction.

Jordan walked home slowly, deep in thought over what he had just witnessed.

Chapter 9

"I've got a plan," Justin announced as he bounded off his front porch the next morning.

"You always have a plan," Jordan said.

"True. It's what great minds do. But I think you're going to be on board with this one as soon as I tell you."

"Well, don't keep me in the dark then."

Justin paused for effect. "I call it Operation M and M."

"Like the candy?"

Justin shook his head. "My plan has nothing to do with candy. It's short for Miller and Math."

"Um, I hate to break it to you, but those two things don't quite go together like chocolate and a candy-coated shell."

"Maybe not now," Justin said. "But they will after Operation M and M is done."

Jordan didn't look convinced. "How does the plan work?"

"I'm still working out a few details," Justin said. "And some of it depends on some cooperation from Mr. Miller."

"Yeah, good luck with that."

"When has one of my plans ever gone wrong?" asked Justin

Jordan looked at him incredulously. "What about Operation Early Dismissal?"

Justin laughed as he remembered his failed plan from third grade. The boys had wanted to see the latest superhero movie that had just come out in theaters. The matinee show started at four and they wouldn't make it in time unless they left school early. Justin had come up with a plan to change the timer for the dismissal bell so it would ring early.

The first part of the plan worked perfectly. Jordan was able to distract Mrs. Rodriguez, the office administrator, by asking her to help with the copy machine. That allowed Justin to sneak into her office. Unfortunately, the second part of the plan didn't go nearly as well. Justin didn't have any idea how the controls for the bell system worked. Instead of setting the dismissal bell to ring thirty minutes early, he accidentally set it to ring every thirty seconds.

Pandemonium broke out in the school as the bell rang repeatedly. Teachers were in the halls trying to figure out what was going on. The principal came running from the teacher's lounge, one hand wiping at a smear of mustard on his shirt from dropping his ham and cheese sandwich. He narrowly avoided plowing into Mrs. Rodriquez who was sprinting from the copy room. The principal began frantically pushing buttons, but the ringing continued. They were finally able to silence the bells by yanking the plug powering the control system.

"We didn't make the movie. Remember?"

"Yeah, that one didn't quite go as planned," Justin admitted. "And Mrs. Rodriquez still gives me a fishy look whenever she sees me. But this plan is foolproof. Phase one is gaining his trust."

Jordan remained skeptical as they continued walking to school. To be fair, Justin's plans were usually amazing. He and Stephanie had come up with a plan to capture the burglars who had been robbing houses in their neighborhood. He had devised the plan to help catch the kidnappers who were holding Mr. Duchesne hostage. More recently, he had figured out a way to sneak into the library in the Maynard House so Stephanie could get a look at a cipher hiding under one of the chairs. Jordan hoped Justin's latest plan would work but getting Mr. Miller to like math seemed like an impossible task.

Surprisingly, Operation M and M got its first opportunity that very morning. The class was reading about eighteenth century inventions. Jordan was not big on reading, but it was cool to read about some of the things first created so long ago. The cotton gin, lightning rod, electric telegraph, and the submarine were all invented in that hundred-year period. The soft drink and the flush toilet also made their first appearances.

While most of the class had their heads down as they read, Justin was keeping an eye on Mr. Miller. He was poking a skinny finger on his calculator and scribbling numbers on a piece of paper. Occasionally, he would write something down in his gradebook. He was scowling as he worked at his desk.

Justin saw the scowl as an opportunity. Risking his teacher's wrath, he rose from his seat and quietly approached Mr. Miller's desk.

"Um, excuse me, Mr. Miller," Justin said.

"What is it?" Mr. Miller snapped.

"I'd be happy to help you record grades if you want."

"What makes you think you'd be any help? It's just a lot of number crunching," Mr. Miller said.

"Number crunching is my middle name," Justin said. "Well, actually it's David, but you know what I mean."

Mr. Miller didn't smile. "And how do you propose to help?"

"Have you considered using a spreadsheet to make

it easier?" Justin asked. "You can calculate averages for each student and even graph their progress across the semester if you want to."

Mr. Miller looked at Justin like he had just grown another head.

"It's pretty easy," Justin said. "Here, let me show you."

For the next thirty minutes, Justin's fingers flew over the keys on his teacher's laptop. He added all the students and entered equations to calculate grades for each subject. Mr. Miller watched with a doubtful eye. When Justin had finished, he showed his teacher how easy it was to enter grades.

"See, all you have to do is put the test grade in this column and the spreadsheet will calculate his overall grade for the subject."

Mr. Miller looked dubious. He looked down at his scribbled calculations and then back at the information on his computer screen.

"Well, it appears to work, but I'll have to do some more checking before I'm confident this is really going to help," he said, then added, "You should get back to your history now."

As he returned to his desk, Justin looked to the back of the room at Jordan, who gave him a thumbs up. Justin hid a smile as he sat down. Phase one of Operation M and M was a success.

Chapter 10

"I haven't seen Jordan or Justin in a week," Stephanie said as she and Catherine sat down to lunch.

"I saw Justin on the way home yesterday," Catherine said. "Jordan is stuck in detention. I still can't believe he got two weeks for trying to help. That's just not right."

Stephanie looked around the cafeteria to make sure no one else was close, then lowered her voice so only Catherine could hear. "Mr. Miller sure sounds like a jerk."

"Mrs. Wilson isn't as good a teacher as Mrs. Gouche, but at least she teaches us math," Stephanie said.

"Yeah, and my dad always finds cool problems for you and me to solve," said Catherine. "Speaking of which, here's what he gave us today."

Catherine pulled a folded sheet of paper from her pocket. The problem was written in Mr. Duchesne's neat handwriting.

What is the number of the parking space which contains the car?

| 16 | 06 | 68 | 88 | | 98 |

Wait! Do you want to try to solve this puzzle before seeing if Stephanie and Catherine can do it? Can you figure out the pattern in the parking lot and determine the number for the parking spot containing the car?

"Looks pretty easy," Stephanie said. "It's just a pattern problem. We just need to figure out the pattern and figure out the missing number."

"Too easy," Catherine agreed. "We should have this done before recess."

Twenty minutes later, the girls were still hard at it.

"This pattern doesn't make any sense," Stephanie complained. "It goes down by ten and then goes up by sixty-two. Do you think he messed up the numbers somehow?"

"Maybe, but my dad usually thinks these things out pretty thoroughly before he gives them to me."

"It must be some kind of complicated pattern then."

"I don't think so. My dad said he almost didn't

give it to me because it was too easy. I guess we'll have to work on this one after school," Catherine said. "There's no way I'm going home and telling my dad we couldn't solve it."

The bell rang, letting them know it was time to get back to class. Both Stephanie and Catherine reached for the puzzle at the same time, knocking it to the floor. Stephanie reached down to pick it up. As she started to hand it to Catherine, she took one more look at the puzzle. She started to laugh.

"What's so funny?" Catherine asked.

"Your dad was right. It's really easy."

"You figured it out?"

"Yeah, I think we were just looking at it wrong." She giggled again and handed the paper to Catherine —upside down!

What is the number of the parking space which contains the car?

Catherine began to laugh along with Stephanie. Her dad was right. The puzzle *was* easy when you looked at it this way.

"We've got to show this to the guys," Stephanie said.

"I bet they don't figure it out."

"I know. It'll drive Jordan absolutely crazy!"

They were still laughing when they got back to their classroom.

They were surprised to see a young woman standing at the front of the room.

"Good afternoon, class. I'm JoElla. I'll be substituting this afternoon," she said. She smiled broadly as she looked at the class.

Dylan raised his hand. "Welcome, JoElla. Mrs. Wilson usually has me fill in substitute teachers on the work we are doing."

"Sweet!" Bill hooted. "No work!"

"Don't listen to him, JoElla. Some people in this class just don't care to learn," Dylan said.

"Well, thank you. And your name is…?"

"Bryce Bookerman, ma'am," he answered, somehow managing to keep a straight face. Behind him, Bryce snickered.

Stephanie shook her head. It was going to be a bad afternoon. Every kid knew there were some unwritten rules substitute teachers were meant to follow. First, never introduce yourself by your first name. Second, never smile at the class. Third, never ever trust a student who says they want to help. JoElla had just violated all the rules. That meant only one thing. The class was going to run over her like a stampede of buffalo.

JoElla looked at Mrs. Wilson's lesson planner. "Okay, this afternoon we'll be doing a social studies worksheet."

Dylan's hand shot up immediately.

"Yes, Bryce?" Another snicker from the real Bryce.

"We finished that yesterday."

"You did?"

"Yes, ma'am."

She consulted the lesson planner again. "And the math homework?"

"Done."

"That's done too?"

Dylan nodded, an innocent smile plastered on his face. Now even Stephanie was stifling laughter.

"We finished that this morning," Dylan said. "I think that's the reason Mrs. Wilson said we could have an extra recess this afternoon."

JoElla looked at the clock. It was almost one o'clock.

"How much time do you usually get for extra recess?" she asked. Stephanie wanted to answer "none, because we don't get extra recess," but she decided to keep quiet and see how this played out.

"Usually an hour and a half," Dylan said.

"An hour and a half?"

"Yes, ma'am, but I don't think you should give us more than an hour because I'm sure the class is anxious to get back to our silent reading."

"Okay, you can have recess until two," JoElla said. The class quickly filed out of the room before she could change her mind.

When Catherine and Stephanie got to the playground, the boys were playing a rowdy game of push tag. It was like tag, but someone only became "it" when they were knocked to the ground. They weren't usually allowed to play this version of the game, but there weren't any teachers to supervise in the middle of the afternoon.

Stephanie grabbed a soccer ball from the rack of playground equipment and began bouncing it on one knee. Catherine watched carefully, then took another ball and tried to duplicate what her friend was doing. She was only able to bounce it once or twice before the ball went off the edge of her leg and fell to the ground. After a while, though, she was able to do it multiple times in a row.

"Nice!" Stephanie said. "Now try your other leg." She switched the ball to her left leg and began bouncing again.

Catherine was concentrating as hard as she could, all of her attention focused on the soccer ball. Once, twice, three times the ball bounced off her knee.

"Look, Stephanie! I got—"

Without any warning, she was slammed to the

ground. The soccer ball went flying. Stunned, Catherine looked up to see Dylan staring down at her.

"You're it!" he yelled triumphantly. Catherine couldn't say a word because all the breath had been knocked out of her.

Stephanie screamed. "We aren't even playing, you jerk!"

Dylan grinned. "Well, it looks to me like you are now. And she's it!" Dylan's friends laughed uproariously. Stephanie helped her friend to her feet, all the while keeping a close eye on Dylan and his friends, who were still bent over in laughter.

"Are you okay?" she asked anxiously.

Catherine, who was still catching her breath, held up a thumb. Stephanie gave a huge sigh of relief.

Catherine took a couple of tentative steps and decided her legs were fine. "I think that's enough recess for one day," Catherine said. She looked angrily across the playground at Dylan as she and Stephanie slowly made their way toward the school.

Chapter 11

"This is surprisingly good, Jordan," Mr. Miller said as he returned Jordan's paper on "The Road Not Taken." Jordan wasn't sure whether or not to take that as a compliment, but he was happy to see the *B+* on the top of the page. *My parents will be even happier*, he thought.

To be honest, it was one of the few times Jordan had felt the least bit proud of a paper he had written. He was used to doing well on all his math and science work, but not so well when it came to writing. He looked through the paper. He still had some misspelled words and Mr. Miller had corrected his grammar in a few spots, but his teacher's comments were all positive. He had even written *Great job capturing the theme of the poem* at the top of the page.

The day got even better when Mr. Miller asked the class to get out their math books. "Today we're going to be working on percentages," Mr. Miller said.

Maybe not the most exciting of math topics, but

it had been three days since they had done any math, so Jordan was still happy. He watched as Mr. Miller went through an example of calculating percentages.

"Let's look at a simple example," he said. "Let's say we want to calculate 30% of 60. We multiply 30 by 60 to get 1800. Then we divide by 100 to get 18."

It was clear that more than half of the class was lost. Hakim summed it up as simply as he could. "Why?" he asked.

"What do you mean, why?"

"I mean, why do you do it that way?"

"Because that's the way you do it," Mr. Miller said.

"But I don't see why that works," Hakim persisted.

"It works because that's the way you do it," Mr. Miller said stubbornly.

"But why?"

"What part of 'that's the way you do it' do you not understand?"

From the front row, Justin could see that Hakim and Mr. Miller were both getting frustrated. Justin understood why the math worked, but looking around the class, it was clear that most of his classmates didn't. This looked like a perfect opportunity for phase two of Operation M and M.

Justin raised his hand. "Maybe you could show them the shortcut you showed Jordan and me." he said.

"What shortcut?" Mr. Miller asked.

"You know, the one for problems like this one. It sure helped me to understand it better."

Mr. Miller looked confused. He had no idea what Justin was talking about. Trying to save face, he handed the marker to Justin.

"Here, you can show them yourself," he said.

Justin went to the board and explained. "Mr. Miller showed us is an easy way to do this." He wrote a different problem on the board.

$$10\% \text{ of } 60 = ?$$

"That's easy," said Hakim. "It's 6."

"Right," Justin said. "And how did you come up with that number?"

Hakim thought for a moment and then said, "You just divide 60 by 10."

"Exactly," said Justin. He added two more equations to the board.

$$10\% \text{ of } 60 = 6$$
$$30\% = 10\% \times 3$$
$$30\% \text{ of } 60 = ?$$

"So what is 30% of 60?" Justin asked.

"18!" said Hakim.

"And how did you get that?" asked Justin.

"Easy. Since 30% is 3 times as much as 10%, I just multiplied 6 by 3."

"Nailed it!" Justin said. He glanced over at Mr. Miller. The teacher nodded for him to continue. Justin noticed that he was jotting down notes on a sheet of paper.

"Here's something else Mr. Miller taught us," Justin said. "You can switch the numbers around and it's still the same. Here's an example." He wrote an equation on the board.

$$32\% \text{ of } 50 = ?$$

"This one isn't as easy, is it?" When Justin saw heads shaking, he continued. "But it gets a lot easier if you switch the numbers around."

$$32\% \text{ of } 50 = 50\% \text{ of } 32$$

"50% of 32 is much easier, isn't it?" He looked over at Robbie. "What do you think, Robbie?"

It was a risky question. If Robbie didn't know the answer, he might get mad, and the consequences wouldn't be good, especially since Robbie was the biggest kid in the class and Justin was the smallest. Robbie thought for a moment and then said, "It's 16, right?" He didn't sound sure of his answer, but he was correct.

"Right! 50% is just half and half of 32 is 16." Justin looked over at the teacher. "Thanks again for the tips, Mr. Miller. I understand it a lot better now."

"Happy to help, Justin," he said, a small smile playing over his lips.

From the back of the room, Jordan looked on in amazement. Justin shot him a smile as he returned to his seat. Phase two of Operation M and M was complete.

***

When Jordan walked out of detention that afternoon, he was surprised to see Justin waiting for him.

"How come you're still here?" Jordan asked.

"I waited so we could talk about the next step in my plan. In the meantime, I helped Old Mike wipe down the cafeteria tables."

"Old Mike" was the school janitor. He wasn't that old, but everyone called him Old Mike, even the students. The Math Kids had helped him get his job back when he had been accused of stealing from student lockers.

"I still can't believe you took over Mr. Miller's lesson like that. I mean, you were really taking a big chance."

"Probably, but it was pretty obvious he didn't know how to explain percentages," Justin explained. "It was worth the risk because it looked like he wanted some help."

"Man, he sure needed it. If he said one more time that that was just the way it works, I think my head would have exploded."

Justin laughed as he pictured his best friend's head blowing up in the middle of one of Mr. Miller's lessons.

"So what's next?" Jordan asked.

"Phase one was to gain his trust by showing him how math can help him with everyday things like keeping track of student grades. Phase two was to help him better understand how the math works. If he's not afraid of math, maybe he won't avoid it so much."

"And what's phase three?"

"Phase three is to get him to find out how much he needs math."

"How are you planning on doing that?" Jordan asked.

"I have no clue. Why do you think I waited for you? Do you have any ideas?"

Jordan shook his head. "Not off the top of my head, but I'll see if I can come up with something."

"Good, because we need that before I can move onto the final phase."

"What's the final phase?"

"The final phase is my little secret, but trust me, you'll know it when you see it."

Chapter 12

On Saturday morning, the Math Kids met for the first time since school had started. They had a lot of catching up to do.

"So Justin gets up in front of the class and teaches them how to do percentages, and Mr. Miller sits in his chair and grins," Jordan said. "I try to teach multiplication and I end up with two weeks of detention. I ask you, where is the fairness in that?"

"Life is cruel, my friend," Justin said. He reached for the last glazed doughnut, only to have Jordan snatch it away at the last second.

"Hey, I was going to eat that," Justin protested.

"Life is indeed cruel, my friend," Jordan said. He stuffed half of the doughnut into his mouth. Glaze covered his lips and small pieces of doughnut dropped onto the floor.

"That is gross, Jordan," Stephanie said. "Funny, but gross."

Catherine asked, "Has Mr. Miller gotten any better?"

"Not much," Justin said, "but we're working on it." He went on to explain Operation M and M.

"Do you really think it will work?" Catherine asked. She sounded doubtful.

"So far, so good," Justin responded. "But we've still got a long way to go."

"How are things with Mrs. Wilson?" Jordan asked.

"She's okay, I guess," Stephanie said.

"That's not exactly a ringing endorsement."

"No, but it's not really her that's the problem," she said.

"Let me guess," Jordan said. "Is it Dylan Carmen?"

Stephanie nodded emphatically. "How can he be such a jerk all the time?"

"It takes practice if you want to be good at something," Justin quipped.

"Well, he's had all the practice he needs if you ask me," she said. "He might even be worse than Robbie, if you can believe that."

"Speaking of Robbie, he's been acting a little weird this year," Jordan said.

"What do you mean?" Catherine asked.

"I mean, he's still kind of a jerk, but he actually thanked me for teaching him how to do lattice multiplication."

"He did not!"

"He did—really!" Jordan answered. "And I think

there's something going on with his dad." He explained what he had seen when he saw Robbie and his dad outside of detention. "Every time Mr. Colson even moved an arm, Robbie flinched like he was about to be smacked."

"Do you think his dad is hurting him?" Stephanie asked.

"Maybe. It could explain why he's always picking on kids smaller than him."

"Which is everyone, especially me," Justin said.

"And there's something else," Jordan added. "Remember that time his arm was in a sling for a week?"

Justin nodded. "Yeah, he said he ran his bike off the road. Do you think maybe it was something else?"

"Maybe," Jordan said. "He seems to have more than his share of accidents. I always just thought he was clumsy, but now I'm not so sure."

"Do you think you should talk to the school counselor about it?" Catherine asked.

Stephanie nodded. "I mean, I don't like Robbie one little bit, but I also don't want to see him get hurt."

"I don't know. I guess I'll have to think about it."

The four sat quietly, thinking about Robbie and his dad. Justin broke the silence. "Well, since there's nothing we can do about it right now, who wants to work on a little math?"

"What do you have in mind?" Jordan asked.

"Catherine and I have a good problem for the two of you," Stephanie said, trying hard to hide her grin. "We've already worked it out."

Catherine handed the parking lot problem to Justin, making sure to hand it to him right-side up.

"Eighty-seven," Justin immediately responded.

"What? How did you do that so fast?" Stephanie asked.

"Superior brain power," he grinned. Stephanie looked doubtful, so he added, "Plus I've seen this puzzle before."

"That's no fair," Stephanie pouted, snatching the paper from Justin's hand.

"If you think that's not fair, wait until you see the problem I brought," Justin said. He reached into his back pocket and pulled out a sheet of paper. Everyone crowded around the paper to read the puzzle.

Albert and Bernard are trying to guess Cheryl's birthday. She gives them a list of ten possible dates:

May 15	*May 16*	*May 19*
June 17	*June 18*	
July 14	*July 16*	
August 14	*August 15*	*August 17*

She whispers the correct month to Albert. She whispers the correct day of the month to Bernard.

Albert: I don't know when her birthday is, but I know Bernard doesn't know either.

Bernard: At first, I didn't know her birthday, but I know now.

Albert: If you know then I do too.

When is Cheryl's birthday?

Wait! Do you want to try to solve this puzzle before seeing if the Math Kids can do it? Can you figure out when Cheryl's birthday is?

"Any ideas on how to get started?" Justin asked.

"I think a table of dates would be helpful," Stephanie said. She drew a table on the whiteboard.

May		15	16			19
June				17	18	
July	14		16			
August	14	15		17		

"Well, we know it's not June 18th or May 19th," Jordan said.

"How?" asked Catherine.

"Because then Bernard would know her birthday since there's only one month with that day."

Catherine thought about that a bit and then nodded her head. "Good call, Jordan." She scratched through those two dates. "Two down, eight to go."

May		15	16			~~19~~
June				17	~~18~~	
July	14		16			
August	14	15		17		

Everyone studied the remaining eight dates.

"I'm stuck," Stephanie said. "Every month has at least two dates and every number is in two different months."

"There must be something in what Albert and Bernard say that'll give us the clues we need," Justin said.

"Let's start with the first thing Albert says then," Jordan said. "I don't know when her birthday is, but I know Bernard doesn't know either."

"I don't think that's much help," Stephanie said. We already know that Albert can't guess by just knowing the month."

"And we've already ruled out May 19th and June 18th because we know that Bernard can't guess the birthday with just the number," Catherine added.

There was silence as everyone stared at the whiteboard. Everyone but Justin, that is. He was also deep in thought, but he was carefully studying the first statement made by Albert.

"I think we missed something very important in what Albert said," Justin told his friends. They looked at him expectantly. "I think the important part is 'but I know Bernard doesn't know either.'"

"But we've already crossed off those dates that Bernard could easily guess," Stephanie countered.

"True, but I think we can cross off three more dates too."

"How do you figure?" Jordan asked.

"Albert says he knows Bernard doesn't know, so that means Albert is sure that Bernard can't guess the birthday with just the number, right?" Justin asked. There were nods all around. "If the month is May, one of the possible dates is May 19th. That means it can't be May, or else Albert wouldn't be absolutely sure Bernard doesn't know."

Justin's statement was a lot to take in, and everyone else took some time to think about it. Finally, Jordan spoke up. "I think Justin's right. If Albert had been given the month of May, he'd know there would be a chance that Bernard could guess.

"That means he also couldn't have been given the month of June," Catherine added, "since Bernard would know if it was June 18th."

Stephanie agreed, "That sounds right, Catherine. So now we can cross off all of the dates in May and June." She updated the table on the whiteboard.

May		15	16			19
June				17	18	
July	14		16			
August	14	15		17		

"Way to go, team," Catherine said. "We're halfway there. Five down, five to go. What's next?"

Jordan said, "Well, Bernard says that he didn't know at first, but now he knows. So he must have figured it out based on what Albert said."

"Good point, Jordan," Catherine said. "Bernard now knows that Cheryl's birthday is in either July or August since he would have eliminated May and June the same way we did. That means it can't be either July 14th or August 14th."

"How come?" Jordan asked.

"Because if the day of the month was the 14th, he still wouldn't know which one it was," she explained. Catherine scratched out those dates.

~~May~~		~~15~~	~~16~~			~~19~~
~~June~~				~~17~~	~~18~~	
July	~~14~~		16			
August	~~14~~	15		17		

"That makes sense, Catherine," Stephanie agreed. "So it has to be either July 16th, August 15th, or August 17th. In any of those cases, the day would give Bernard everything he needs to know her birthday."

"Yeah, but what about Albert?" Justin asked. "In his last statement he said he now knows her birthday too."

"That's right, Justin," Jordan said. "So that means it can't be August 15th or August 17th, since just knowing it was August wouldn't be enough information for Albert to be sure when her birthday is."

"If we cross those dates out, it only leaves July 16th," Stephanie said. "We did it!"

~~May~~		~~15~~	~~16~~			~~19~~
~~June~~				~~17~~	~~18~~	
July	~~14~~		16			
August	~~14~~	~~15~~		~~17~~		

"Let's check the clues to make sure," Justin said. He was a stickler for checking his work, so no one was surprised when he suggested this.

"Okay," Stephanie said. "Let's do it. If we're right, Albert was given July for the month and Bernard was given 16 for the day. Albert couldn't guess because there are two dates in July. Bernard couldn't guess since he wouldn't know if it was May 16th or July 16th. That checks out so far."

"But," Catherine continued, "if Bernard is able to narrow the months down to July and August based on what Albert said, then he can easily guess the only date left with the 16th is July 16th. And, if Bernard is able to guess, Albert knows the date can't be the 14th. Since he knows the month is July, the only date left is July 16th."

"Everything checks out!" Justin said happily. "I love it when a plan comes together!"

"Yeah, if only our people problems could be solved so easily," Jordan said.

Chapter 13

On Wednesday morning, Jordan was still thinking about Robbie and his dad. "Hey Mom, can I ask you a question?" he asked.

His mom looked up from her phone. "Sure, Jordan. What can I help you with?"

"I saw something at school the other day that kind of bothered me." That statement got his mom's full attention. "I saw a dad picking up his son and it looked like the kid was really afraid of him."

"What made you think that?"

"Well, every time the dad moved his arm, the boy ducked like he was about to be hit," Jordan said.

"I'm glad you told me about this, Jordan. There may not be anything to it, but it also could be a sign of abuse. Have you talked to the boy about it?"

"No. We're not exactly the best of friends. To be honest, he's kind of a bully. He's always getting in fights and pushing people around."

Jordan's mom nodded as she listened. "Sometimes,

when kids are abused, they redirect their anger on others, usually those who are smaller and weaker than them."

"'Yeah, that sounds about right with this guy," Jordan said.

"Who is this boy?"

Jordan didn't answer right away. He didn't want to get Robbie in trouble if he had misread what had happened outside of the school.

"Um, I'm not sure I should tell you yet."

"I understand. But I want you to know that this could be very serious. Have you talked to the guidance counselor?"

Jordan shook his head.

"Think about that. And you need to let me know if you see anything else that concerns you. Will you do that?"

"I will, Mom," Jordan said. He looked over at the clock. "I'd better get going or I'm gonna be late for school."

As he walked to school, Jordan thought back to the scene he had witnessed between Robbie and his dad. Was he making too big a deal of it? Had he just imagined Robbie flinching when his dad raised his hand?

As he rounded the corner leading to the school, Jordan saw a police car pull over to the curb. He watched as Robbie got out of the car and slammed the door behind him. Robbie looked upset. He stared after the car as it drove away. Then, instead of heading toward the school, he crossed the street and walked into a small park. Under normal circumstances, Jordan would have avoided a confrontation and continued on his way to school. Today, something made him do just the opposite. He crossed the street and entered the park. He spotted Robbie sitting on one of the swings. His head was down, and Jordan was surprised to see that Robbie was crying.

"Hey, Robbie!" Jordan called out. Robbie looked up and saw it was Jordan.

"What do you want?" Robbie asked. He wiped quickly at his eyes. His mouth was twisted into a sneer. But Jordan noticed something else. There was a red mark on the side of Robbie's face. Maybe it was just his imagination, but the mark looked like a fading handprint.

"Just being friendly, dude," Jordan said. He hoped it came out casually even though he was nervous.

"Yeah, sure," Robbie said doubtfully.

"Hey, it's none of my business, but—"

"You're right. It is none of your business," Robbie snarled.

"It's just that you looked kind of upset when you got out of your dad's car," Jordan began.

"So? What's it to you?" Robbie said sharply.

Jordan settled into one of the swings. He remained silent, not sure how to proceed. Robbie finally broke the silence.

"My dad was mad and gave me a little slap," he said. "It's not a big deal. It's what parents do, you know?"

"No, it isn't," Jordan said.

Robbie looked at him warily.

"Parents aren't supposed to do that," Jordan continued. "Seriously, they're not."

"Oh, I get it," Robbie replied. "You're telling me your perfect parents have never gotten mad and punished you?"

"Not like that," Jordan said. "I've been punished, but they don't hit me."

"Not even a spanking?"

"Not that I can remember," Jordan said. "They usually take away my video games or make me do extra chores."

"That sucks," Robbie said.

"Yeah, but it doesn't leave a mark," Jordan said.

The two boys sat in silence on the swings.

"Well, I guess I'd better get to school," Jordan finally said. He couldn't think of anything else to say. He felt bad for Robbie, but he wasn't sure what he should do about it. He also wasn't sure how Robbie would react if he tried to help.

"Yeah, me too," Robbie said. "I don't need to get in any more trouble with Miller the Killer."

"He's a real pain, isn't he?"

"You don't know the half of it," Robbie said as he rose from his swing. "He gave me another week of detention."

"What for this time?" Jordan asked.

"I complained about my grade on the math homework. I used Justin's tips on percentages and I'm sure I got most of them right, but he still gave me an *F*."

"Mr. Miller stinks at math. You probably got more right than he did."

"Yeah, try telling that to my dad," Robbie said. "I think he was madder about my grade than I was."

The boys walked the short distance to school, both deep in thought. There was a moment of awkwardness as they entered the front door. Robbie looked up and down the hallway. Jordan figured he was checking to make sure none of his friends saw the two talking.

"I've got to get a few things from my locker," Robbie said.

"Yeah, I've got something I need to do too," Jordan said.

Robbie didn't acknowledge, he just walked on ahead. Then he stopped to look back at Jordan. "See you in class," he said.

"Yeah, see you in class," Jordan answered.

He watched Robbie walk down the hallway, then walked in the opposite direction. He took a deep breath outside the door marked *Mrs. Guidry— Guidance Counselor*. He pulled the door open and stepped inside.

When Jordan entered his classroom thirty minutes later, he was surprised to see the principal sitting at Mr. Miller's desk.

"What's up?" he whispered to Justin.

"I don't know," Justin whispered back. "Mr. Miller was here but then he got a phone call and stormed out of the room. The next thing I knew, Mrs. Arnold showed up."

"Is she going to be our substitute teacher today?"

"No, I think she's just filling in until a sub arrives," Justin said. "Where have you been, anyway?"

Jordan never got a chance to answer. "Jordan, can you please take your seat?" Mrs. Arnold said.

The substitute never showed up, so Mrs. Arnold returned to her roots as a teacher and filled in until lunch. Mr. Miller was back when Jordan and Justin returned from recess, and his normally pale face was red with anger.

"In your seats—now!" he barked. The class quickly took their seats. "Take out your social studies books and read chapters six through nine," he said. "And I don't want to hear a sound out of anyone!" For a change, there was no talking back, no groaning, not even a single whisper from the back of the room.

Mr. Miller settled behind his desk and pulled a stack of papers from a large manilla envelope. Justin watched as he studied each piece of paper.

The rest of the afternoon passed without incident. Mr. Miller barely looked up when the dismissal bell rang. While Justin was waiting for Jordan to gather his things, he watched his teacher out of the corner of his eye. Mr. Miller was still looking at the papers spread across his desk, occasionally jotting down a note on a yellow legal pad.

When the other students had left, Justin and Jordan approached their teacher's desk. "Is everything okay, Mr. Miller?" Justin asked.

If looks could kill, Mr. Miller's icy stare would have struck Justin down on the spot. "No, everything is not okay," he said without further explanation.

"If there is anything we can do to help, all you have to do is ask," Jordan chimed in.

"This isn't a math problem. It's a serious legal issue and I doubt a couple of fifth graders are going to be much help."

"Sometimes a fresh pair of eyes can see things a little differently," Justin said. His thoughts went to the parking lot problem, which seemed hard at first but became much easier when you looked at it from a different perspective.

"Look, this is something I need to handle myself," Mr. Miller said.

"Are you sure?" Justin asked. "If I learned anything in the last year, it's that a team of people can accomplish a lot more than just one person."

Mr. Miller said, "If you absolutely need to know what's going on, I'll tell you. My son was pulled over for speeding and reckless driving. I don't think he did it because he's always been a careful driver, but if he's found guilty, he may get sixty days in jail and have to pay a ten thousand dollar fine."

"Wow, that's a lot of money," Jordan said.

"I'm more worried about the jail time," Mr. Miller said.

"Of course, that's even worse," Jordan quickly added.

"Look, we may just be kids, but we were able to help the FBI solve a crime from fifteen years ago. It wouldn't hurt for us to at least take a look, would it?" Justin asked.

Mr. Miller looked at the papers spread across his desk and then at the two boys standing in front of him. His eyes misted a little as he remembered his own son at that age. That thought was enough to change his mind.

"Okay, what do you want to see?"

Chapter 14

As soon as he got home, Jordan called an emergency meeting of the Math Kids. The team gathered in his basement. After Justin and Jordan explained the circumstances, the four friends got down to work.

Mr. Miller had provided them a copy of the police report. The first thing Stephanie noticed was that the arresting officer was none other than Mr. Colson, Robbie's dad.

"There's some payback for you," Jordan said after she'd pointed it out.

"What do you mean?" asked Catherine.

"Mr. Miller gives Robbie an *F* on his math homework and then Mr. Colson arrests Mr. Miller's son."

"The timing seems just a little too convenient, doesn't it?" said Justin.

Jordan thought back to his conversation with

Robbie. "It sure does," he said. "When I was talking with Robbie, he said he thought his dad was madder about his grade than he was."

"Wait! When did you talk to Robbie?" Justin asked. This was certainly news to him.

"This morning. I'll fill you in later. For now, let's see what we can find to help Mr. Miller's son."

For two hours, they read and reread the copy of the police report. Two hours and they had absolutely nothing to show for it.

"Why did you think we would be able to find something if Mr. Miller couldn't?" Stephanie asked.

The Math Kids were taking a break, partly because they were frustrated with their lack of progress and partly because Jordan's mom had brought out slices of chocolate cake and a pitcher of cold milk.

"Yeah, this isn't like the last time when we were able to help solve a math puzzle," complained Justin. "There's no math here."

Jordan was quiet as he finished scraping the last bit of icing from his plate. Justin said there was no math in the report, but Jordan also knew that math seemed to show up in a lot of strange places. Was the team missing something? Jordan picked up the police report and reread one section for what seemed like the twentieth time.

"Wait a minute," he blurted out. Everyone looked over at him. "What if there is some math in here?"

"Where?" Justin challenged. "Officer Colson saw a car driving at high speed and pulled the driver over. He arrested Mr. Miller's son for speeding and reckless driving."

"Justin's right," Catherine agreed. "I don't see any math there either."

"There are numbers," Jordan argued, "and where there are numbers, math can't be far behind."

Everyone laughed, but Justin looked skeptical. "Show me the numbers," he said.

Jordan looked back over the police report, searching for the numbers he had seen. He found what he was looking for in Officer Colson's statements.

"'The suspect's vehicle went past me at the intersection at an estimated 60 miles per hour,'" Jordan read. "There's a number for you."

Justin snorted.

"And here's another number," he said, continuing to read from the report. "'After 10 seconds, the light changed to green and I began following the suspect's car.'"

Now everyone looked skeptical, but Jordan persisted.

"There's also a picture," he said, pointing out the

diagram the police officer had drawn to indicate the position of the vehicle when he pulled it over.

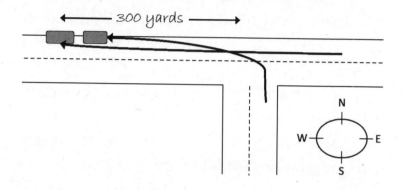

The figure showed where the police car had started and where it had pulled the car over.

"300 yards," Jordan said. "There's another number for you."

"But where's the math?" Justin asked. "60 miles an hour. 10 seconds. And this, it's just a picture showing where the car was pulled over."

Stephanie was looking at the picture intently. She whispered something to Catherine, who started writing furiously in her notepad. She showed the notepad to Stephanie. Both girls looked at each other, and broad smiles spread across both of their faces.

"Okay, spill it you two," Justin said. "What did you just figure out?"

"Well, first of all, Jordan was right," Stephanie said. "There is definitely math here."

Catherine nodded vigorously in agreement. "There is a problem though," she chimed in. "The math doesn't add up."

Justin and Jordan looked at each other. What had the girls discovered that they were missing?

"Let me show you the problem by giving you an example," Catherine said. "You have twenty minutes to complete a round trip up to the top of a mountain and back down. You start at the foot of the mountain. The road to the top is 10 miles long. The mountain is steep, so you only average 30 miles an hour on the way up. How fast do you have to go on the way down to average 60 miles an hour for the entire trip?"

Jordan grabbed a sheet of paper and he and Justin huddled over it for a few minutes.

Wait! Do you want to try to solve this puzzle before seeing if Jordan and Justin can do it? You average 30 miles per hour on the 10-mile road up a mountain. How fast do you need to go on the way back to average 60 miles per hour for the whole trip?

"Wait a minute!" Jordan said. "There's something wrong here."

Catherine smiled. "Oh, really?" she asked innocently.

"Yeah," Justin chimed in. "You would think the answer would be 90 miles an hour since the average of 30 and 90 is 60, but that doesn't work."

"This is a trick question, isn't it?" Jordan asked.

"Yeah, it kind of is," Catherine said.

Stephanie joined in the fun since she knew Catherine had tricked the boys. "If you go 60 miles per hour, that's 1 mile every minute. To go 20 miles, the whole trip would take 20 minutes, right?"

The boys nodded in agreement.

"But if you drive 30 miles per hour that's 1 mile every 2 minutes. To drive the 10 miles to the top, it would take 20 minutes just to get to the top," Stephanie said.

"So that means it doesn't matter how fast you drive on the way down," Jordan said. "You've already used up all of your time on the way up."

"That's right," Stephanie said.

"But what does that have to do with the police report?" Justin asked.

Catherine showed her calculations. Jordan and Justin reviewed her work and agreed. Something *was* wrong with the police report. Like Catherine said, the math didn't work out.

"Mr. Colson said he was stopped at the intersection when the car drove by at 60 miles per hour," Catherine said.

"And he didn't start following the car until the light changed 10 seconds later," Stephanie added.

Catherine showed her calculations that the car had gone 293 yards during that 10 seconds.

"That means the car was 293 yards ahead of the police car before Mr. Colson even started chasing him," said Stephanie.

"But Mr. Colson said the car was pulled over 300 yards from the intersection," Catherine added. "It really doesn't matter how fast the police car went. There is no way the police car could have caught the car at that spot with that big a lead."

The girls were right. The police report was wrong.

"Maybe Mr. Colson wrote down the wrong location for where he pulled the car over," Justin ventured.

"We could check that out," Jordan said. "There's a picture of the car pulled over. It's right in front of a billboard for the new hotel in town."

"But what if Mr. Colson got the amount of time he waited before he started chasing the car wrong?" Justin asked.

"He might have," Stephanie said. "But even so I don't think the math works out."

"What do you mean?" Justin asked.

"Well, let's say it was really only 5 seconds instead of 10. That means Miller's car would have only been 150 yards ahead of the police car."

"That's a big difference," Justin said.

"But, if Miller was going 60 miles an hour, the police car would have to travel twice as fast to catch him at that spot. That's 120 miles an hour. And that doesn't take into consideration that it would take him some time to get up to that speed and some time to slow down to a stop."

"Yeah, the math is wrong again, isn't it?" Justin agreed.

Jordan was nodding his head thoughtfully. "But if we're right and the math doesn't work, what does that mean?"

"I'll tell you what I think it means," Stephanie said. The other kids looked at her in anticipation. "I think it means Mr. Colson was lying in his report."

"I bet it's because he was trying to get back at Mr. Miller for giving Robbie a bad grade," Jordan said.

"So, what do we do next?" Catherine asked.

"Well, first I think we need to check out the numbers," Jordan said. "We need to find out exactly where he pulled over Mr. Miller's son."

"And if the numbers check out?"

Jordan smiled. "Then I guess I was right about there being math in the report, wasn't I?"

***

The next night, Jordan got the perfect opportunity to check the numbers.

"Who wants pizza for dinner?" Mrs. Waters asked.

"Me!" Linda shouted from the top of the stairs.

"Me too!" Jordan yelled from his spot in front of the TV.

"Me three!" Mr. Waters joined the chorus.

"Sounds like pizza it is then," Mrs. Waters said. "Next question: Pizza World or Happy Pizza?"

That question did not get a unanimous response. Linda wanted Happy Pizza. Mr. Waters preferred Pizza World. Jordan paused his show and thought about the math that didn't add up. "Let's try that new place, A Slice of Heaven," he suggested.

"That's a little out of the way, isn't it?" his mom asked.

"Not really," Mr. Waters answered. "We can just take Watson over to Main." Jordan smiled. Main Street was where Mr. Miller's son had been pulled over. They'd have to drive right past the spot.

"I'll ride with you, Dad," Jordan volunteered. His mother raised an eyebrow. It wasn't often that Jordan would volunteer to do anything when he was in the middle of watching a show.

Ten minutes later, they came to the intersection Mr. Colson had described in his police report. As he

and his dad waited at the red light, Jordan watched the cars go past. He tried to estimate the speed the cars on Main Street were going. As the light changed, he picked the last car that had gone through the intersection and watched it. He was surprised to see how big a lead it had by the time his dad made the left-hand turn onto the street. When they passed the sign for the new hotel, the car was still well ahead. By then, Jordan had forgotten all about the pizza his dad was picking up for dinner. He couldn't wait to get home to tell the other Math Kids what he had learned.

Chapter 15

The Math Kids went to school early the next morning. They wanted to catch Mr. Miller before the rest of the class arrived. The front door to the school was locked, but Old Mike let them in when he heard them knocking. The janitor looked down at his watch.

"This is early, even for you," he said with a smile.

"Thanks for letting us in, Old Mike," Justin said. "Do you know if Mr. Miller is here yet?"

"I haven't seen him, but the lights are on in his room, so I suspect he is. Are you trying to get bonus points for coming in early?"

"No, this is important business," Jordan said.

"Then I'd better let you get to it," the friendly janitor said. "Good luck with whatever it is you're up to this time."

The four rushed down the hallway and burst into the room, startling Mr. Miller as he sipped coffee from a travel mug. Luckily, the plastic lid kept the hot coffee from spilling on him as he dropped it on the desk.

"I think we've got it, Mr. Miller!" Jordan announced loudly.

"Got what?" Mr. Miller said in irritation.

"Proof that your son didn't do anything wrong," Justin said.

Mr. Miller stared at the four kids. He looked doubtful, but there was a trace of hope in his eyes.

"Well, don't keep me waiting. Show me what you found," he said.

Catherine and Stephanie went through their calculations, writing the equations on the board as they talked. To help explain, Justin told his teacher the example of the car going up the mountain. Jordan told him about his trip to the pizza restaurant and how Robbie had said his dad was really mad at Mr. Miller. All four were breathless with excitement when they finished.

"This is all very interesting," Mr. Miller said, "and I appreciate the work you've put in, but I don't think this is going to help."

For a moment, the Math Kids were completely deflated. They had worked hard to prove their case, but Mr. Miller made it clear it was all for nothing.

Jordan was not willing to give up yet. "But the math proves Mr. Colson wasn't telling the truth," he protested.

"It still ends up being my son's word against that of a police officer," Mr. Miller said sadly. "And I'm afraid that's not going to go well."

"What are you going to do, Mr. Miller?" Stephanie asked quietly.

"The attorney is going to try to get the charges reduced, but he's afraid that's all we're going to be able to do. The court date is next week, so we don't have a lot of time." Mr. Miller looked at the clock. "Speaking of time, if you don't mind, I'm supposed to call the attorney for an update."

The Math Kids walked out into the hallway to give the teacher some privacy for his phone call.

"Well, that didn't go like I expected," Catherine said. "I thought he'd be really excited we were able to show Mr. Colson was lying."

"Maybe he's right though," Stephanie said. "It's hard to argue against a police officer. I wish there were another way we could prove our case."

"Maybe there is," Justin said. "In fact, this might be a case where we can kill three birds with one stone."

"What's your plan, Justin?" Stephanie asked.

"I don't think I have enough time to explain right now," Justin said.

Jordan said, "Okay, then let's meet in the library after school. You heard Mr. Miller—we don't have much time to act if this goes to court next week."

The hallway was beginning to fill with kids heading to class. Jordan saw Robbie slowly limping down the hall toward his locker.

"Morning, Robbie!" Jordan called out.

Robbie started to raise a hand in response but noticed Bill Cape was looking in his direction. He quickly lowered it and put a sneer on his face. "Are you talking to me, loser?" he asked. Bill laughed.

Stephanie shook her head, torn between getting mad at Robbie and feeling sorry for him. She and Catherine turned to go to their classroom, crossing to the other side of the hall to give Robbie a wide berth. As they passed him, they heard Bill Cape ask him about his limp.

"It's no big deal," Robbie answered. "Just twisted my ankle a little when I stepped off a curb."

"What a wimp," Bill said.

"I still have two good fists," Robbie threatened.

Stephanie and Catherine gave each other a knowing look.

***

The Math Kids met in the school library when the dismissal bell rang that afternoon. Old Mike shook his head as they passed him at the doorway.

"You kids can't get enough of school today, huh?" he said. "In early and now staying late. When I was your age, I couldn't wait to get out of school at the end of the day."

"And now you spend even more time in school, don't you?" Jordan said.

Old Mike shrugged his shoulders. "What can I say? Maybe school is growing on me."

When they were alone, they huddled around one of the reading tables.

"So, what's your plan, Justin?" Jordan asked.

"The way I see it, we have two things to do," he explained. "First, we need to get the charges dropped against Mr. Miller's son. Second, we need to find a way to stop Mr. Colson from hurting Robbie. I think if we do both of those things, we might just have a chance to successfully complete Operation M and M."

"Even the final phase?" Jordan asked.

"Even the final phase," Justin answered confidently.

"What's the final phase?" Catherine asked.

"He won't tell me," Jordan said. "But he said I'd know it when I see it."

Stephanie shook her head. "Okay, fine. So, we'll ignore Operation M and M for now," she said. "How do you propose doing the other two things, getting the charges dropped and helping Robbie?"

"We offer up a trade," Justin said.

He explained what he was thinking, then sat back and waited for reaction from the other Math Kids.

"It sounds a little risky to me," Catherine said. "How can we be sure he'll agree to the trade?"

"He has to," Justin answered. "Remember, the facts, and the math, are on our side."

"Maybe," Jordan said, "but I agree with Catherine. This could be risky for Robbie. I already took a big chance when I talked to the counselor, but this could make it even worse."

"What do you think, Stephanie?" Justin asked.

"I agree with you, Justin. The math doesn't lie, even if Mr. Colson does. I say we do it."

Justin looked at Jordan and Catherine.

"I guess I'm in too," Jordan said.

"I'll make it unanimous, then," Catherine said.

"Okay, I think it's time for the Math Kids to take a trip to the police station," Justin said.

Chapter 16

The police station was an imposing stone building on Fourth Street. Jordan, Justin, and Stephanie had been here once before when they were in fourth grade. They had met with Detective Ponnath to talk about the burglars who had been robbing houses in their neighborhood. It turned out the burglars had tried to fool the police by picking their targets using prime numbers, but the Math Kids had been able to figure out the pattern and determine where they were going to hit next. They had alerted Mr. Colson, who was able to catch the burglars in the act.

When they walked into the building, they were greeted by the desk sergeant, an older man with wispy white hair wearing a rumpled blue uniform.

"What can I do for you kids?" he asked.

"Is Officer Colson here?" Justin asked.

"He sure is. I think he's at his desk." He pointed across the room.

Justin took a deep breath and led the way. When they reached Mr. Colson's desk, he was busily tapping away on his laptop. His desk was a mess, with stacks of papers scattered everywhere. He didn't look up as they stood in front of his desk.

"Um, excuse me, Officer Colson?" Jordan said. The policeman looked up, annoyed by the interruption at first but then smiling as he recognized them.

"The famous Math Kids," he said. "Catchers of burglars and finders of lost treasure. What can I do for you?"

Catherine was confused. She had never met Robbie's dad and expected him to be more like his son.

"Is there a place we can talk in private?" Jordan asked.

Now Mr. Colson frowned. He crossed his arms across his chest and his eyes squinted. Catherine was amazed by how he had changed his whole image in a matter of seconds.

"We can talk right here, son," he said gruffly.

"I don't think we should though," Jordan said, not backing down from the stern look.

"You don't, huh? Fine, follow me then." Mr. Colson rose from his desk and led them across the room, moving briskly around the desks and file cabinets that occupied much of the space. Justin had to almost run to keep up with him. Even Jordan, with his much longer legs, had to walk quickly.

"I'll be in interrogation room two, Frank" he called out to the desk sergeant.

Catherine looked over at Stephanie when she heard their destination. Her friend was tugging at her ponytail. Mr. Colson ushered them into a small room with a single metal table in the middle. The table was bolted to the ground, as were the metal chairs, two on each side of the table. Mr. Colson closed the thick door with a loud clunk. Catherine noticed a camera mounted near the ceiling in one corner. Its blinking red light went out as Mr. Colson flipped a switch on the wall.

"What's the camera for?" Catherine asked.

"It's for recording confessions," Mr. Colson said. "You got something you want to confess?"

"Um, no sir," she replied, wishing he had kept the door open and the camera turned on.

Mr. Colson sat in one of the chairs. Jordan and Justin sat across from him, but the girls remained standing. Catherine looked longingly at the closed door.

"You called this meeting," Mr. Colson said gruffly. He squinted his eyes toward Jordan. "What's so secret that it couldn't be said at my desk?"

Jordan swallowed. His mouth suddenly felt very dry and he wished he had stopped for a drink of water at the fountain near the front door.

"Um, uh…" he stammered.

"Well, out with it," Mr. Colson barked.

Jordan froze. He couldn't get the words out. The policeman rose from his chair. "I guess we're through here," he said.

"No, we're not," Stephanie said firmly.

"Oh, so one of you can actually speak," Mr. Miller said sarcastically. "Okay, little lady, what do you have to say?"

"We don't think you were accurate with the police report on Mr. Miller's son," Stephanie said. She looked directly at the police officer as she said it. He tried to stare her down, but she refused to look away.

"Miller's kid was speeding and driving recklessly," Mr. Colson said.

"And you just happened to be there when he did it?" Stephanie asked.

"Sometimes you get lucky," the officer replied.

"Or did you know it was Mr. Miller's son from the very beginning? Like before you even pulled him over?" Jordan asked.

Mr. Colson's face turned red. "I don't need to listen to this," he said. He rose from his chair and headed toward the door.

"We have evidence," Catherine said.

That statement stopped Mr. Colson at the door. "Evidence of what?" he asked. "How could you possibly have evidence? None of you were even there!"

"No, but we have proof anyway," Catherine said. "Undeniable proof."

"And the next two people to see it are your captain and the judge," Justin said.

Mr. Colson looked at the four kids. "You're bluffing," he said. "I don't think you have any proof."

The Math Kids stared right back at him. "Then call our bluff," Justin said.

Mr. Colson was fast. One second, he was standing by the door and the next he was gripping Justin's arm. He yanked upward, lifting the boy off the ground. Justin cried out in pain.

"Put him down!" Stephanie yelled.

"Or what?" the policeman sneered.

"Or we show the captain the recording," she said.

Mr. Colson glanced into the corner. The red light on the camera was blinking. He looked over at the door, where Catherine stood by the switch.

"Okay, okay," he said, releasing Justin's arm. "Turn off the camera and we'll talk."

Catherine flipped the switch, and the red light went out.

"Have a seat," Mr. Colson said to Catherine.

"I can listen from here," she said, keeping one hand close to the switch.

Mr. Colson sank into his seat. "What do you want?" he asked.

"We're willing to offer you a trade," Justin said.

"A trade? A trade for what?"

"Two things," Justin said. "First, you're going to

say you made a mistake when you pulled Mr. Miller's son over. Can you do that?"

"Yeah. I was just trying to scare Miller so he'd quit picking on my son," Mr. Colson said. "I'll deep-six the arrest."

"Deep-six?" Jordan asked.

"Yeah, deep-six. You know, make it go away forever. Geez, don't you kids know anything these days?"

"Math," Jordan said.

"What?" Mr. Colson looked confused.

"You asked if we know anything. We know math," Jordan said. "And you know what? If *your* math was better, we probably wouldn't have caught you lying on the report." At the door, Catherine put one hand over her mouth to keep from laughing at Jordan's smug expression.

"You're a little smart aleck, you know that?" Mr. Colson said, his face flushing as he started to rise from his chair.

"Ahem," Catherine said. Mr. Colson looked at her and saw her finger was on the switch for the camera. He sank back down into his seat.

"Fine. I'll take care of the report. What else?" he said.

Jordan took a deep breath. This was the tough one.

"Well?" Mr. Colson demanded.

"It's about Robbie," Jordan said.

"What about him?" Mr. Colson asked. He suddenly sounded very defensive.

"He shows up at school sometimes with bruises," Jordan said.

"So? What can I say, he's a big clumsy kid."

Another deep breath. "I think maybe it's more than that, Mr. Colson," Jordan said.

Mr. Colson shot to his feet. In an instant, Catherine flipped the switch, and the red light began blinking. He glared angrily, then sighed and sat again.

"You can talk to us, or we'll have to share what we know with the captain," Stephanie said.

"I've already talked with Mrs. Guidry," Jordan added.

"Who's that?" asked Mr. Colson.

"She's the guidance counselor at our school," Jordan answered.

"Are you kidding me?" Mr. Colson asked angrily. "You know that she..." His voice trailed off as it sank in.

"Yes, she has to report any suspected child abuse to authorities," Jordan said. "That means it's going to come out anyway, but I think it would be better if you own up to it and start making changes."

Mr. Colson took several deep breaths. "Look, he

gets a little mouthy sometimes, you know, talking back and stuff. Ever since his mom walked out on us, it's just been the two of us. I'm trying to hold down a job, get dinner on the table, get him to school. All that stuff by myself. You don't know what it's like. It gets hard sometimes." He looked down at the table, tears coming to his eyes.

At that moment, Jordan felt a little sorry for him. Mr. Colson was right. He *didn't* know what it was like. He had two parents who shared the responsibility for everything. When there were problems, they worked them out together. Out of nowhere, the Robert Frost poem jumped into his head. *Maybe sometimes we don't have an option on which road to take*, Jordan thought. But he also remembered what he had concluded about the poem. Whatever road you ended up taking, you had to make it your own. Mr. Colson had to be responsible for his actions, regardless of his situation.

"So, what do you want?" Mr. Colson asked.

"I think you and Robbie should talk to a counselor to work out your problems," Jordan said.

"You want me to go to counseling?" Mr. Colson asked. "Unbelievable."

"But remember, we're offering you up a trade," Justin said.

"What do I get out of this?"

"We'll get Robbie moved to another teacher so he can have a fresh start," Justin said. "That means he won't have to deal with Mr. Miller anymore."

"That's your deal, huh?" Mr. Colson said. "It sure seems like I'm giving up a lot more than you're offering. What if I don't agree to this lousy trade?"

"Then we go to the captain," Stephanie said firmly.

"You're not really giving me a choice then, are you?"

"We are," Jordan said. "A Hobson's choice."

Chapter 17

The charges against Mr. Miller's son were dropped without any fanfare. The explanation given by the policeman was "equipment failure." He claimed his radar gun had malfunctioned, giving him a false reading for the car as it drove past him at the intersection. Mr. Miller didn't care why the charges were dropped. He was just relieved his son was no longer facing a large fine and possible jail time.

"It's not a perfect solution," Jordan said, "but I think it's the best we could get under the circumstances."

"What's not perfect about it?" Justin asked.

"Well, Mr. Colson covered up his first lie with another one. He won't get in any trouble at work."

"True, but I don't know if losing his job would help Robbie," Justin said.

"We are going to tell Mr. Miller we were the ones that got the charges dropped, aren't we?" Jordan asked Justin as they walked to school the next day.

"We have to," Justin replied. "We promised Mr. Colson that we would get Robbie moved to another room, remember? I think Mr. Miller will make that happen, and if we're lucky, he'll also help with the final phase of Operation M and M."

"Are you ever going to tell me what the final phase is?"

"I already told you. You'll know it when you see it."

At lunchtime, Justin and Jordan stayed behind while their classmates headed to the cafeteria.

"Can we talk to you for a few minutes, Mr. Miller?" Justin asked.

Mr. Miller smiled. It wasn't something he did much in the classroom, so the boys were glad to see the corners of his mouth turn up.

"I had a feeling you two had something to tell me," he said.

"Why do you say that?" Justin asked innocently.

"Because, out of the blue, the charges against my son were dropped. You don't happen to know anything about that, do you?"

"We might have helped just a little," Justin said.

"Or maybe a lot!" Jordan chimed in.

"I figured as much," Mr. Miller said. "Did your math help?"

"In a way it did, but it wasn't what got Mr. Colson to change his mind," Justin said.

"And I suppose you can't tell me what happened, can you?" Mr. Miller asked.

Jordan looked over at Justin, who shook his head.

"No, sir," Jordan said.

Mr. Miller looked thoughtfully at the two. "I guess that's alright," he said. "I do want you to know that I appreciate anything you did to help. If there is anything I can do to return the favor, all you have to do is ask."

Jordan looked over at Justin again. This time, Justin nodded.

"Well, there is something," Jordan said.

Mr. Miller smiled again. "I figured as much," he said. "What can I do?"

They explained that Mr. Colson would like his son to have a fresh start for fifth grade. Mr. Miller understood and agreed that would be good for everyone. He said he would talk to the principal about getting him moved.

"It might take a few days to get things worked out, but I think she'll agree to the change. Anything else I can do?" he asked.

Jordan said, "No sir. Thanks for your help."

"No, Jordan, thanks for yours. You and your friends taught me a great lesson—and not just about math."

"But we did teach you a little math, didn't we?" Justin asked.

"Just a little," Mr. Miller smiled. "But it's a long year. Maybe you can teach me a little more."

"That sounds great!" Jordan said.

"Okay, you guys better get to lunch."

Jordan and Justin were walking toward the cafeteria when Justin suddenly stopped.

"I forgot something," he said. "Go on without me. I'll be there in a couple of minutes."

Justin walked back into the classroom while Jordan watched him, a look of curiosity on his face.

At lunch a few minutes later, Jordan asked him what he had forgotten.

"Oh, just something to do with phase four," his friend said.

"You know, I'm beginning to think there is no such thing as phase four. I think you just made it up to mess with me."

"Oh, there is definitely a phase four," Justin said. "Like I told you—"

"—I know, I know. I'll know it when I see it."

"You got it, buddy." Justin smiled and took a large bite of his sandwich.

Chapter 18

The following Monday, Jordan was in a great mood as he and Justin walked to school. The weather was perfect. The sky was bright blue without a cloud in sight. And for the first time this year, he couldn't wait to get to school. On Friday, Mr. Miller had been full of surprises. First, he gave Jordan and Justin some weekend homework—in math! The problems weren't quite as hard as some of the ones Mrs. Gouche had given them, but it was definitely a step in the right direction. Even more surprisingly, Mr. Miller had also announced he was going to be separating the class into math groups beginning the next week. Jordan's jaw had dropped when he heard this.

"Man, I can't wait for math groups," Jordan said.

"I know, it's gonna be great," Justin said.

"I guess it will be just the two of us in our group."

"Maybe," said Justin noncommittedly.

"You think he'll stick someone else in our group?"

"I guess we'll have to see."

When they got to the classroom, they immediately saw that something else had changed. The nametags had been removed from the desks.

"Now that I know everyone's name," Mr. Miller said, "feel free to sit wherever you want."

Jordan looked at Justin and they immediately headed for two desks next to each other.

"Sweet!" Jordan said.

"It looks like Robbie got moved to a different class," Justin noticed.

"I'm glad Mr. Miller was able to make that happen."

"It turns out he was able to get a few other things done too," Justin said.

Justin pointed toward the door. Jordan watched as Catherine and Stephanie entered the room. He remained speechless as the two took the two desks behind theirs.

Justin grinned.

"Phase four?" Jordan asked.

"See, I said you'd know it when you saw it," Justin said.

"Okay, let's get started," Mr. Miller said. "What do you say we start with math today?"

"Yes!" Jordan said.

"Since Jordan seems so enthusiastic about the

idea, we'll let him pick a spot for his math group," Mr. Miller said.

Jordan looked around him. "I think we're already where we want to be."

Epilogue

Three weeks later, the Math Kids were talking on the playground during recess when Dylan Carmen approached.

"What is this, a nerd convention?" he asked.

The four friends decided to ignore him and went back to their discussion on a particularly tricky math problem Mr. Miller had given them that morning.

"Hey, I'm talking to you!" Dylan said, raising his voice.

"Do you need something, Dylan?" Stephanie asked.

"Yeah, I want to know why you two get special treatment."

"I don't know what you're talking about," Justin said.

"Shut up, pipsqueak," Dylan said. "You know exactly what I'm talking about. Your girlfriends got bonus points on their tests and now get to move to another class. I'm getting tired of it."

Now Dylan was standing right in front of the

Math Kids. Justin saw that the bigger boy's fists were clenched, and his face was red with anger. *Here we go again*, Justin thought.

"Look—" he began.

"No! You look!" Dylan said as he raised a fist towards Justin. The four friends drew closer together in solidarity.

"I've got this." Robbie stepped in between Dylan and the Math Kids. Justin watched in surprise.

"What's your problem, Robbie?" Dylan demanded.

"No problem with me, Dylan. And let's keep it that way, okay?" Robbie said. Justin noticed that Robbie remained calm and didn't raise his voice.

"I don't know, Robbie," Dylan said. He glared angrily. "I think maybe you and I might have a problem."

Dylan pushed Robbie. He stumbled backward but kept his feet. Justin was sure that a fight was about to break out, but Robbie only smiled.

"I'm not going to fight, Dylan. Not that I couldn't pound you into the ground if we did, but it would be stupid. We'd both end up getting detention, and where's the fun in that?"

Dylan didn't know what to do. Robbie remained calm throughout the confrontation. He never raised his voice. Dylan was expecting a fight and all he was getting was a discussion.

"Um, yeah, I guess that makes sense," he finally said.

"You wanna play some wallball?" Robbie asked.

Dylan said, "Yeah, sure."

Robbie and Dylan walked away. Robbie stopped and turned back toward the Math Kids. You could have knocked Justin over with a feather as he gave the four a wink before turning his head and walking away.

The End

Appendix

Child Abuse

An Incorrect Solution brings up the very serious subject of child abuse. In the book, the abuse occurs in a single parent household, but abuse can occur in *any* kind of family regardless of race, class, or family circumstances.

The Mayo Clinic (www.mayoclinic.org) describes child abuse as follows:

Any intentional harm or mistreatment to a child under eighteen years old is considered child abuse. Child abuse takes many forms, which often occur at the same time.

- **Physical abuse:** Physical child abuse occurs when a child is purposely physically injured or put at risk of harm by another person.
- **Sexual abuse:** Sexual child abuse is any sexual activity with a child, such as fondling, oral-genital contact, intercourse, exploitation, or exposure to child pornography.

- **Emotional abuse:** Emotional child abuse means injuring a child's self-esteem or emotional well-being. It includes verbal and emotional assault —such as continually belittling or berating a child—as well as isolating, ignoring, or rejecting a child.

- **Medical abuse:** Medical child abuse occurs when someone gives false information about illness in a child that requires medical attention, putting the child at risk of injury and unnecessary medical care.

- **Neglect:** Child neglect is failure to provide adequate food, shelter, affection, supervision, education, or dental or medical care.

In many cases, child abuse is done by someone the child knows and trusts—often a parent or other relative. If you suspect child abuse, report the abuse to the proper authorities.

A child who's being abused may feel guilty, ashamed, or confused. He or she may be afraid to tell anyone about the abuse, especially if the abuser is a parent, another relative or family friend. That's why it's vital to watch for red flags, such as:

- Withdrawal from friends or usual activities
- Changes in behavior—such as aggression, anger, hostility, or hyperactivity—or changes in school performance
- Depression, anxiety or unusual fears, or a sudden loss of self-confidence
- An apparent lack of supervision
- Frequent absences from school
- Reluctance to leave school activities, as if he or she doesn't want to go home
- Attempts at running away
- Rebellious or defiant behavior
- Self-harm or attempts at suicide

Specific signs and symptoms depend on the type of abuse and can vary. Keep in mind that warning signs are just that—warning signs. The presence of warning signs doesn't necessarily mean that a child is being abused.

If you suspect one of your classmates is being abused, it is important to tell someone— your teacher, parent, guidance counselor, or another trusted adult.

Girls Think of EVERYTHING

Stephanie was reading a book called *Girls Think of EVERYTHING: Stories of Ingenious Inventions by Women*, written by Catherine Thimmesh and illustrated by Melissa Sweet. This book is full of interesting stories of inventions by women, including chocolate chip cookies (Justin's favorite), windshield wipers, and the ReThink app, which can alert you to potentially harmful words before you send a message. It's a great read for everyone!

The Prisoner's Dilemma

The cooperation game the class played is an example of an area of mathematics known as game theory, the study of mathematical models of cooperation and conflict. Game theory is also used in economics, political science, computer science, and psychology.

One of the most famous cooperation/conflict "games" is known as the prisoner's dilemma. The concept was developed by Merrill Flood and Melvin Dresher, two American mathematicians, in 1950. Albert Tucker, a Canadian mathematician, set down the rules of the game and named it the "prisoner's dilemma." The prisoner's dilemma is laid out as follows:

Two members of a criminal gang are arrested and put in prison. The prisoners don't have any way of communicating with each other. The police don't have enough evidence to convict them for the charge of robbery (which has a three-year prison sentence), so they hope to convict both on the lesser charge of breaking and entering (which has a one-year prison sentence).

The police offer each prisoner a choice: they can either remain silent and not cooperate or they can betray the other prisoner.

- If A and B each betray the other, each will serve 2 years in prison
- If A betrays B but B remains silent, A will be set free and B will serve 3 years in prison (and vice versa)
- If A and B both remain silent, both will serve 1 year in prison

There are four possible combinations:

	A silent B silent	A silent B betrays	A betrays B silent	A betrays B betrays
A punishment	1 year	3 year	Set free	2 year
B punishment	1 year	Set free	3 year	2 year
Total	2 year	3 year	3 year	4 year

If A remains silent, he will receive either 1 year or 3 years in prison (an average of 2 years). If A betrays, he will either go free or receive 2 years in prison (an average of 1 year).

Based on this, the best decision for A is to betray.

Unfortunately, that's also B's best decision, which means both will betray and each will receive 2 years in prison, a total of 4 years between them.

The best "team" decision would be for both to remain silent and serve 1 year in prison, a total of 2 years between them.

The Vasa

The Vasa set sail on her maiden voyage on August 10, 1628. At the time, she was the most powerfully armed warship in the world, with sixty-four bronze cannons. Twenty minutes into her journey, the ship was hit by two strong winds. It leaned to port, water poured in, and the ship sank less than a mile into its first voyage. Thirty people died.

The ship was raised more than three hundred years later and is now on display in its own museum in Stockholm, Sweden. Because the ship sank in the cold, oxygen-poor water of the Baltic Sea, it was protected from the bacteria and worms that usually destroy wooden wrecks. About ninety-five percent of Vasa's wood was intact when it was raised in 1961. That provided archeologists and engineers a golden opportunity to study Vasa and determine why it sank.

The engineers found two primary reasons. First, the ship was built using two different rulers. One side was built using a twelve-inch ruler and the other with an eleven-inch ruler. That meant one side of the ship was heavier than the other side, causing it to lean to one side.

The second reason it sank was that the ship was top-heavy. Too much of the ship's weight was nearer to its top. Why is this a bad thing? The stability of a ship depends on the center of gravity and the center of buoyancy. The center of gravity is the point where you could suspend an object and it would remain balanced. The center of buoyancy is the center of gravity of the water displaced by the ship. For a ship to be stable, the center of buoyancy should be above the center of gravity of the ship. In other words, we want more of the overall weight of the ship to be underwater. In the case of Vasa, the center of gravity was above the center of buoyancy, making the ship unstable.

Do you want to try an experiment to see this for yourself?

Here's what you'll need:

- Pan or bowl to hold water
- Disposable paper cups
- Modeling clay
- Straw

Here's how to try this out for yourself:

- Fill the pan halfway with water
- Cut the paper cup to about 1 inch high to act as your boat
- Put some modeling clay in the bottom of your boat and float the boat on the water
- Put the straw into the clay (as close to the center of the boat as possible)
- Take a small amount of clay and roll it into a ball
- Place the ball at different positions on the straw (closer to the bottom, halfway up, at the top)

Questions to ask:

- What position of the clay makes your boat the most stable (less likely to tip over)?
- How does moving the clay ball affect the center of buoyancy?

Other Ways to do Multiplication

One of the cool things about math is that there are often lots of different ways to solve a problem. The lattice method described in the book is one way to multiply multi-digit numbers. This method is also known as the Chinese method, Italian method, gelosia multiplication, and several other names because it has been used in many different cultures for hundreds of years.

John Napier, a Scottish mathematician, created a manually operated calculator in 1617 that was based on lattice multiplication. It used rods made of bone, so it became known as Napier's Bones. This calculator was important at the time because very few people could multiply numbers bigger than 5.

You can make your own calculator using paper or stiff cardboard to create the rods. First make a table that is ten squares across and nine squares down. In the first column, write the numbers from 1 to 9. After the first 1 in the top row, write the numbers from 1 to 9. For each square, multiply the number at the top with the number on the left. If the number is less than 10, put a 0 in the upper left side of the square.

1	1	2	3	4	5	6	7	8	9
2	0/2	0/4	0/6	0/8	1/0	1/2	1/4	1/6	1/8
3	0/3	0/6	0/9	1/2	1/5	1/8	2/1	2/4	2/7
4	0/4	0/8	1/2	1/6	2/0	2/4	2/8	3/2	3/6
5	0/5	1/0	1/5	2/0	2/5	3/0	3/5	4/0	4/5
6	0/6	1/2	1/8	2/4	3/0	3/6	4/2	4/8	5/4
7	0/7	1/4	2/1	2/8	3/5	4/2	4/9	5/6	6/3
8	0/8	1/6	2/4	3/2	4/0	4/8	5/6	6/4	7/2
9	0/9	1/8	2/7	3/6	4/5	5/4	6/3	7/2	8/1

You've probably noticed that this is just the multiplication table!

Cut out the ten vertical strips of numbers. We can now use these to multiply numbers.

Let's say we want to multiply 6 × 425.

First select the strip with the numbers from 1 to 9. Next to this, put the strip with 4 at the top. Do the same with the strip with 2 at the top. Finally, put the strip with the 5 at the top. When you are done it should look like this:

1	4	2	5
2	0/8	0/4	1/0
3	1/2	0/6	1/5
4	1/6	0/8	2/0
5	2/0	1/0	2/5
6	2/4	1/2	3/0
7	2/8	1/4	3/5
8	3/2	1/6	4/0
9	3/6	1/8	4/5

We are multiplying 425 by 6, so we will use the row starting with 6.

Just like we did with the lattice multiplication, we will add up the numbers in the diagonal columns to get the answer. In the rightmost diagonal, there is only one number (the 0), so that is the last digit in the answer.

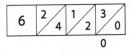

Now add the numbers on the next diagonal.

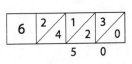

Continue with the other diagonals, working right to left. Carry any numbers greater than ten.

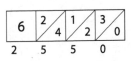

The answer to 6 × 425 is 2,550. And all we had to do was to add a few numbers!

"The Road Not Taken" by Robert Frost

This is a real narrative poem written by Robert Frost. It was published in 1916 and remains one of his most popular works.

> Two roads diverged in a yellow wood,
> And sorry I could not travel both
> And be one traveler, long I stood
> And looked down one as far as I could
> To where it bent in the undergrowth;
>
> Then took the other, as just as fair,
> And having perhaps the better claim,
> Because it was grassy and wanted wear;
> Though as for that the passing there
> Had worn them really about the same,
>
> And both that morning equally lay
> In leaves no step had trodden black.
> Oh, I kept the first for another day!
> Yet knowing how way leads on to way,
> I doubted if I should ever come back.

I shall be telling this with a sigh
Somewhere ages and ages hence:
Two roads diverged in a wood, and I—
I took the one less traveled by,
And that has made all the difference.

The Jury

Part of this book is loosely based on a true story. I once served on the jury in a court case involving a motorcycle, a van, an insurance company, and some math that didn't quite work.

The driver of the motorcycle was suing the insurance company. His claim was that he was riding his motorcycle when he passed a van at an intersection. A short time later, he said the van ran him off the road, wrecking his motorcycle and sending him to the hospital with multiple injuries.

The insurance company claimed there was no van and the man had veered off the road and wrecked his own motorcycle. If there was a van involved, the insurance company would have to pay more money. If there was no van, the man was at least partly to blame, and the insurance company wouldn't have to pay as much.

But where's the bad math?

As I listened to the testimony, I drew a picture of where the van was supposed to be, how fast the motorcycle was traveling, and where the accident occurred (similar to the picture from the police report the Math Kids examined). When we went into the jury room to deliberate on the case, I drew that same sketch on the whiteboard in the room. I told my fellow jurors I didn't believe there was a van involved. I explained the van would not have had time to reach the spot where the accident occurred unless it was traveling well over 150 miles per hour. I showed my calculations to the other jury members.

Did I convince the jury? Unfortunately, not. In civil cases in my state, you only need nine of the twelve jurors to decide a case. I convinced two other jurors with my math, but the other nine sided with the motorcycle driver and the insurance company lost the case.

Maybe the insurance company should have called me as a witness instead of having me on the jury.

Coming Next!

The Triangle Secret
Book 6 in **The Math Kids** *Series*

by

David Cole

Chapter 1

Jordan Waters gave a contented sigh as he looked around his fifth-grade classroom. He felt like things were finally back to normal. The school year had started off very badly. Jordan and Justin Grant, his best friend since kindergarten, had been put into one class. The other half of the Math Kids, Stephanie Lewis and Catherine Duchesne, had been placed in Mrs. Wilson's class. To make matters even worse, Mr. Miller, their new teacher, had made it quite clear he was not a fan of anything having to do with math.

Luckily, the Math Kids had been able to use their math skills to prove that Mr. Miller's son had been falsely accused of reckless driving. To return the favor, Mr. Miller had pulled a few strings and got Stephanie and Catherine moved into his class. The Math Kids were reunited, and things were right with the world. Mr. Miller had put them in the same math group, and now they had time to work together on difficult math problems. There was nothing better than a tough math challenge as far as Jordan and his friends were concerned.

This time the problem came from Catherine's dad. He taught math at the college and had even written some of his own math books. The Math Kids had helped to rescue him when he had been kidnapped. Mr. Duchesne wrote a secret message that could only be solved by using the Fibonacci series, a famous math pattern. Mr. Duchesne knew that they loved math and always had a new problem for them to solve.

"Okay, here we go," Catherine said. "The new ice cream store has sixteen flavors of ice cream. How many ways can they make a three-scoop ice cream cone? The order of the scoops doesn't matter, just the flavors that end up in the cone."

"So two scoops of chocolate and one scoop of vanilla is the same no matter how you stack them up?" Stephanie asked.

"That's right."

Justin nodded. He knew that was an important thing when it came to the number of possible combinations. But he also knew that how you stacked up an ice cream cone made all the difference in the world. Obviously, you would put the vanilla scoop in between the two chocolate scoops!

Stephanie made her way to the white board. She had the best handwriting, so she usually ended up being the one who wrote the group's thoughts down.

"We could do it the hard way," Jordan said. "We could write down all of the combinations and count them, but I have a feeling there's an easier way."

"I think you're probably right," Catherine said. "My dad is usually trying to teach some lesson when he gives us a problem like this. I think we should make a table and see if we can come up with a pattern."

Stephanie started a table on the white board.

Flavors	Possibilities	Combinations
1	1	aaa

"I used letters for the flavors," she said. "The first one is pretty easy. Boring, but easy."

"I don't know," Justin said. "A three-scoop chocolate ice cream cone doesn't sound boring to me."

"We probably shouldn't do ice cream problems right before lunch," Jordan said. The other Math Kids laughed.

"Okay, back to work," Stephanie said. With the help of her friends, she filled out the next few rows in the table.

Flavors	Possibilities	Combinations
1	1	aaa
2	4	aaa, aab, abb, bbb
3	10	aaa, aab, aac, abb, abc, acc, bbb, bbc, bcc, ccc
4	20	aaa, aab, aac, abb, abc, acc, bbb, bbc, bcc, ccc, aad, abd, acd, add, bbd, bcd, bdd, ccd, cdd, ddd

"Wow, the number of possibilities really goes up fast with each new flavor," Catherine said. "It will take us forever if we have to keep writing down all of the possible combinations. Does anyone see a pattern yet?"

The four friends stared at the board, hoping something would jump out at them. Stephanie jotted some numbers on a sheet of paper, then just as quickly scratched them out in frustration. Jordan spent his time trying to figure out the number of possible combinations for five flavors of ice cream, hoping the extra piece of information would allow him to figure out the pattern. Justin closed his eyes, trying to get into his "zone." When he got into the zone, he usually came out with an answer, but this time he came up blank.

Catherine looked at the sequence of possibilities: 1, 4, 10, 20. There was something familiar about the numbers, but she couldn't quite put her finger on it. She and her dad loved mathematical patterns and she had learned about many of them. She was sure this was one of the patterns she had come across.

The lunch bell rang, interrupting their thoughts. Normally, Justin couldn't wait for lunch, but this time he looked back longingly at the board as they walked out the door. He knew the answer was there, but where was it?

They put the problem out of their minds as they ate lunch. Instead, they discussed Catherine's art show.

"Are you entering one of your sketches?" Stephanie asked.

"I'm trying something a little different this time," she said.

Stephanie eyes widened. In her opinion, Catherine was a great artist, but Stephanie had never seen her do anything but sketches. "What are you doing?" she asked. "Painting?"

"I thought about that. I have been reading a book about Wassily Kandinsky. He was a pioneer of abstract art."

"Anyone can do that," Justin interjected. "It's just shapes that don't make any sense. In my opinion, if I can do it, it's not art."

"I think you'd actually like Kandinsky," Catherine retorted.

"I doubt it."

"What if I told you his art was full of math?" Catherine asked.

"Okay, that might make it a little more interesting."

"He used shapes—especially circles and squares—in most of his works. It is amazing to see how much expression he could get out of such simple shapes."

"How can you get expression out of a square?" Justin asked. His look said he wasn't buying it.

Stephanie ignored Justin. "So you're doing an abstract?" she asked.

"No, but I am using shapes. But unlike Kandinsky, my entry is going to be three-dimensional. I'm going to..."

Catherine grew quiet as she suddenly remembered where she had seen the pattern they had just been looking at. She smiled because she was sure she knew how to solve the problem.

Before she could say anything, though, Jordan's phone buzzed. He pulled it out of his pocket and stared wide-eyed at the screen while his friends looked on.

"Your art project is going to have to wait," he said tensely. "I just got a text from Agent Carlson. He's in trouble!"

Chapter 2

Two days earlier...

FBI Special Agent Bob Carlson stepped out of Terminal 3 at Cairo International airport and was immediately hit with a blast of hot, dry air. It was mid-morning, and the temperature was already in the low nineties. Carlson removed his suit coat and draped it over one arm. He loosened his tie and looked around, searching for the contact he was supposed to meet.

"Agent Carlson?"

Carlson looked to his right and saw a small, dark-skinned man wearing a pair of white pants and a loose-fitting cotton shirt. The man gave Carlson a brief bow and extended his hand.

"Mr. Hassan?" Agent Carlson asked.

"Mahmood Hassan," the man responded with a wide smile. "It is an honor to greet you, Agent Carlson." Another short bow.

"The honor is mine," Carlson replied.

"This way, sir. My car is just over here." Hassan

motioned toward a four-door sedan parked with one tire up on the curb. It was dented and so dusty it was difficult to determine the color underneath. Hassan opened the trunk and Carlson stowed his small suitcase.

When Carlson was seated, Hassan started the car and darted into traffic, narrowly missing being hit by a taxi. The driver honked loudly as he swerved out of the way. Hassan laughed and waved.

"I really appreciate you picking me up. I could have rented a car," Carlson said.

"That is a very bad idea, Mr. Carlson. The traffic is quite horrible and Cairo drivers follow laws that are both numerous and unwritten."

Hassan passed a car on the right, veering onto the shoulder before swerving back onto the road in a cloud of dust.

"See, that was quite all right," Hassan smiled. "It was, as we say, a bite of zucchini."

Hassan laughed at Carlson's confused look.

"I think you would say a piece of cake."

Carlson chuckled, but clutched the door handle as Hassan changed lanes again without bothering to look to see if a car was in the way. Another horn blast as a truck steered to the left just in time.

"And I thought driving in Washington DC was dangerous," Carlson said.

"No worries, my friend," Hassan said. "As a great Imam once said, 'My heart is at ease knowing that what was meant for me will never miss me, and that what misses me was never meant for me.'"

Carlson was happy to finally arrive safely at his hotel. Hassan quickly hopped out of the car and retrieved Carlson's bag from the trunk.

"I'll give you some time to get settled in," Hassan said. "I'll pick you up first thing in the morning and we'll go to the pyramids."

"How far away are they?"

"Only fourteen kilometers, but with traffic we should plan on one hour," Hassan said. "I'll be outside at seven o'clock."

"That'll work perfectly. I'll see you then, Mr. Hassan."

"Please, call me Mahmood, sir."

"Only if you call me Bob."

"Thank you, Bob, sir." Hassan gave another bow and got back into his car. He pulled into traffic, horns blaring.

Thirty minutes later, Carlson had checked in, showered, changed his clothes, and was ready to explore. He was only in town for two days, and he wanted to see as much as he could in that short time.

He hailed a taxi and directed the driver to the Khan Al Khalili market. Carlson spent an enjoyable two hours looking through the medieval-style mall with its spice dealers, gold merchants, and everything else a person might want to purchase. He haggled with a merchant for a small Aladdin-style metal lamp. The shop owner wanted two hundred and fifty Egyptian pounds, but Carlson bargained him down to one hundred and twenty-five, about eight US dollars. He stopped for lunch, enjoying kushari, a mix of noodles, rice, black lentils, fried onions, and tomato sauce, while he watched the tourists pass by.

He asked a merchant for directions to the Cairo corniche, an area Hassan had recommended to Carlson because of its great views of the Nile river.

"Dok Dok dock," the vendor told him, pointing down a twisted row of shops.

"Dock dock dock?" Carlson asked.

The man laughed. "Yes, Dok Dok is the name. It's a dock, you know, like a landing for boats. It's in Garden City."

"Oh, that makes more sense."

He walked toward the river and was able to secure a ticket on a felluca, a traditional wooden sailing boat, that was headed in the right direction. The ship was about to set sail when two burly men hopped aboard just in the nick of time. They wore identical blue striped kaftans, the traditional loose-fitting outerwear worn by many Egyptian men. With dark, thick beards, they could have passed for twins.

Under a stiff breeze, the felucca made good time while Carlson enjoyed the view. It was a rare instance of relative quiet in a city of twenty million people. When the ship docked forty minutes later, Carlson found his way to the Museum of Egyptian Antiquities. He walked through rooms filled with mummies of ancient kings, enormous statues, boats, coffins, and artifacts from the pyramids. He was admiring the Gold Mask of Tutankhamun, made of almost twenty-five pounds of gold, when he noticed the two men from the boat.

They were standing just inside the entrance to the room. They were conspicuously looking at nothing, just standing against a wall. They turned quickly when Carlson glanced their way, pretending to examine a blue vase adorned with a large image of a cat. Something signaled an alert in the back of Carlson's brain and he decided it was time to leave. Outside the museum, he sat on a bench behind a short row of bushes. He peered through the foliage but didn't see the men exit. *It's probably nothing*, he thought to himself.

Carlson took a short walk to a restaurant Hassan had suggested. He was able to get a table with a nice view of the Nile as dusk settled. Bab El-Sharq restaurant served many traditional Egyptian dishes and Carlson selected a few his new friend had recommended. Shish tawook was chicken cooked on a skewer and served with rice and pita bread. He had a large glass of qamar al-din, a delicious drink made from apricot juice. Dessert was umm ali, a light pastry topped with powdered sugar and shredded coconut.

When dinner was finished, he took a taxi back to his hotel. The streets were crowded with people. His taxi driver had to slam on his brakes several times to avoid hitting pedestrians who had strayed off the sidewalk. He drove with one hand on the steering wheel and the other on the horn. Carlson was glad the ride was short because the incessant honking was starting to give him a headache.

He paid the driver and entered the hotel. He took a glance outside and saw two bearded men in blue-striped kaftans leaning against the wall across the street.

Well now, this is starting to get interesting, he thought to himself as he waited for the elevator.

Acknowledgements

"Math. It's just there... You're either right or you're wrong. That's what I like about it."
—Katherine Johnson

Katherine Johnson was the main character in the movie *Hidden Figures*. Her work in orbital mechanics—alongside fellow female African American females Dorothy Vaughan and Mary Jackson—was instrumental in putting astronaut John Glenn into space in 1961. There are other famous African American mathematicians like Mark Dean, who invented the first gigahertz computer chip and Elbert F. Cox, the first black man to earn a Ph.D, not just in the United States, but in the entire world. Mae Carol Jameson, a mathematician, engineer, physician, and astronaut, was the first African American woman to visit space. And we can't forget Lonnie Johnson, a famous mathematician and inventor who holds more than 120 patents, including the Super Soaker and Nerf Gun.

Mathematics doesn't care where you came from, your skin color, or your gender. As Katherine Johnson said, "It's just there…" My thanks to all the mathematicians out there. I appreciate your hard work, inspiration, and your journey down the path of discovery.

Thanks to Common Deer Press for helping me to follow my passion for math and writing. Maybe it's a niche market, but I think it's important and I really appreciate Kirsten and her team for helping me to live out my dream. I hope their faith is justified.

Shannon O'Toole—what can I say? You're amazing. One of my favorite things in the whole publishing process is receiving that email from you that says you've completed the illustrations. I know next to nothing about art, but I do know enough to recognize great talent when I see it.

I love to hear from my readers. You can contact me at www.TheMathKids.com.

Stephanie, Jordan, and Justin—You are my life. I hope I make you as proud as you make me.

And last but never least, thanks to my wife Debbie for thirty-five years! No marriage is without its struggles, but those little bumps are so small compared to the amazing peaks.